STORIES FROM THE REGISTRY

--A HEARTWARMING TALE OF ONE FAMILY'S SOJOURN OVER EIGHT GENERATIONS--

CARL F. VERGE

STORIES FROM THE REGISTRY

Copyright © 2015 by Carl Verge

All rights reserved. This book or any portion thereof may not be reproduced or used in any manner without the express written permission of the publisher
except for the use of brief quotations in a book review.

ISBN: -13-978-1517213282

ISBN: -10-1517213282

Book Cover – The register at the Priory in Christchurch, UK

 Photo by Stephen Verge

Graphs by Peter Warr

Table of Contents

CHAPTER ONE: NICHOLAS AND THE PRIORY

CHAPTER TWO: BECOMING CITIZENS

CHAPTER THREE: MARRIAGE OF JARMAN AND MARY

CHAPTER FOUR: THE CHILDREN OF JARMAN AND MARY

CHAPTER FIVE: THE MYSTERY OF THE BOYS' PARENTS

CHAPTER SIX: NICHOLAS' FIRST MARRIAGE

CHAPTER SEVEN: JOY AND SORROW

CHAPTER EIGHT: NICHOLAS' SECOND MARRIAGE

CHAPTER NINE: ELIZABETH AND MARY

CHAPTER TEN: BEYOND CHRISTCHURCH

CHAPTER ELEVEN: THE DEATH OF SARAH

CHAPTER TWELVE: THE ULTIMATE WEDDING

CHAPTER THIRTEEN: SHORTENED LIVES

CHAPTER FOURTEEN: THE END OF AN ERA

CHAPTER FIFTEEN: THE LURE OF THE OCEAN

CHAPTER SIXTEEN: JOHN AND HONORA MEET

CHAPTER SEVENTEEN: THE STORM

CHAPTER EIGHTEEN: A GREAT TRAGEDY

CHAPTER NINETEEN: A CHILD AT CHRISTMASTIME

CHAPTER TWENTY: THE SECOND GEORGE

CHAPTER TWENTY ONE: A DIFFICULT DEPARTURE

CHAPTER TWENTY TWO: DEEP THOUGHTS

CHAPTER TWENTY THREE: CRIME AND PUNISHMENT

CHAPTER TWENTY FOUR: AN UNEXPECTED EVENT

CHAPTER TWENTY FIVE: SETTLING IN THE NEW LAND

ACKNOWLEDGEMENTS

I am grateful to all who helped me in the writing of this book. First of all I deeply appreciate the work of my wife, Marion, who edited every page many times. She was also a great source of encouragement and patiently spent many hours alone as I created this book. I prefer that the writer of this book be "us" instead of "me".

THIS BOOK IS DEDICATED TO MY WIFE, MARION.

Our children and grandchildren have also been very supportive in this endeavour. I give credit to our grandson Peter Warr who created charts for the book, our son Stephen for his research and the photo on the book cover, and our daughter Cindy who gave me a subscription that put me on the road to ancestry.

I deeply appreciate the archivist of the Priory in Christchurch, Debra Elund, who provided Stephen and me with the original records of our ancestors back to 1696. She also read my book with great detail to see how accurately it depicted life in Britain at that time. I also thank her for her kind endorsement.

Lisa Higgins Verge, a very renowned author not only wrote me an endorsement, but also coached me through the whole process of publishing the book. I was advantaged by her expertise, and her willingness to share it with me is deeply appreciated.

Rev. Cal Morgan read the document and was of great help in applying his professional editorial skills to the document. He also wrote a very encouraging endorsement.

Many thanks to our good friend Ruth Whitt who did a masterful job at thoroughly proof reading the final draft of this book.

I appreciate the many Verges that showed interest and support in our Verge Generations Facebook group. During the writing of this book, we were able to find over five hundred Verge descendants from all around the world.

I am grateful to my nephew, the Honorable Wade Verge, Speaker of the Newfoundland and Labrador House of Assembly, who wrote the foreword in this book. I not only sincerely appreciate his comments on the book, but also feel honored by his kind personal remarks.

My sources for the Verge records are very diverse. I received the information through various types of research and from others who were searching our genealogy. I especially recognize John Montgomery, Nancy Hodgson and Bill Verge, who laid the foundation for much of my research many years ago. I am a member of Wikitree and Ancestry, and have gleaned information from both of them. My sources for the way of life in Britain over the four generations were from previous studies that I had done, plus public domain information from my library and the Internet.

FOREWORD

Most of us have spent some time wondering about our ancestry. Where did my family come from? Why did my grandparents make this place their home? How did the earlier generations provide for their families? What kind of struggles did they encounter? How did they overcome adversity and persevere through the harsh times?

We have given passing thought at intermittent times to these questions during our youth. However, as we creep further up the age continuum the need to more accurately connect with our family history takes a more prominent place in our thinking. Still, the questions remain unanswered and the nagging need to know continues to exist. "Stories from the Registry" will connect you with your roots in a way that is insightful, respectful and meaningful. It may very well satisfy your need to know.

Dr. Carl Verge had humble beginnings. Having been born to Joseph and Catherine Verge in the very small rural town of Southern Arm in Green

Bay, Newfoundland, he resisted formal schooling until he reached the age of seven. With an eager mind, a slate to write on, and a chunk of wood to help keep the fire going, Carl began his education in a little one room school. His exceptional abilities resulted in swift advancement through the grades and before too long Carl found himself standing in front of his own class of students and sharing his knowledge with them, some of whom were much older than he was at the time. From school teacher to school board coordinator to College President, Carl thrived on each new experience. As a lifelong learner he eventually earned a PhD from New York University and proceeded to share his educational values and vision with the world. Having travelled more than 40 countries and spoken in hundreds of venues, Dr. Verge has successfully shared his leadership abilities and lifelong experiences with thousands of people.

It doesn't matter if your last name is King, Bennett, O'Reilly, or Barbour. It is insignificant if you are from Hants Harbour, Placentia Bay,

Bonavista Bay, or St. John's. Knowing who you are and where you are from still begs the question, where did it all start? "Stories from the Registry" will tease your mind with exciting possibilities. Based in historical research, this book satisfies our need to know in a way that sparks the imagination with creative stories about our ancestors. We are made to feel the solitude of early life even with all of its challenges. We can feel the uncertainty as people wrestle with infectious disease and we can hear the groaning when another family member succumbs to the inevitable. The winds rage, the waters swell, the nausea of sea sickness takes control of the body but the mental resolve is sufficient to fight the storm and journey on to a new land and a new beginning. The births, deaths, love affairs and weddings come alive with emotion as the connection to our past is skillfully made in this fascinating work of prose. It is a page turner, it is a glimpse into the possibilities, it is a connection to our roots and it is a satisfying answer to the question many of us ask: where did I come from?

Wade Verge, B.Sc., B.Ed., M.Ed.
Speaker, Newfoundland and Labrador House of Assembly

PREFACE

This book is fiction, based upon the records of the births, marriages and deaths of the Verge descendants. The names and dates are real, but the essence of the book goes beyond records and attempts to let the readers experience what everyday life was like as one generation followed another for some three hundred years. I have had a keen interest in the Verge ancestry for some twenty years but never reached the place of writing a book until recently. The primary source of information for the Verges of the seventeenth and eighteenth centuries is a series of records kept in the Priory Church in Christchurch, England. In October of 2013 our son Stephen and I spent time there, checking the Verge records in Christchurch and vicinity. It was a very significant moment when the archivist showed us the original record of the marriage of Nicholas Verge and Elizabeth Scott on December 23, 1696. During that visit, I also became aware of the connection between the Priory and the early generations.

I have reviewed a number of books on genealogy and observed ways in which writers portray information about their ancestors. Some make a list of birthplaces, births, marriages and deaths from the records that they have obtained. This is excellent information for readers and they are excited to find their lineage. Other writers, who have few records, write novels based upon whatever information they have which also makes for a good read. I commend writers who use either of these methods and have enjoyed their writings.

My approach is a mixture of both which I define as the imaginative approach. I became convinced that the only way to enter into the lives of earlier generations was to develop an imaginative framework which makes the records come to life. Every record has a story that waits to be told. I found that the best way to bring those records to life was to research their historical settings and intertwine them in a way that would produce an imaginative but credible book. For example, marriage and wedding stories are based upon the research of their times, including the type of dress, the custom of fall weddings, the frequency of pregnancy before marriage, the throwing of wheat for good luck, the approval of parents, and the magnificence of the Priory as a wedding venue. The records of the births revealed the frequency of childhood deaths and in cases such as these, I researched the diseases that coincided with the deaths and created stories that depicted the sorrow and agony of parents as they watched their children die. For the children that escaped the diseases, I researched the availability and effectiveness of their schooling, their entertainment, clothing, friendships, and home life. When fathers and mothers died early, I studied the context of their deaths and how the children survived. Other research included the types of work available, the political impact upon the citizens, the way in which they entertained themselves and how they went about their everyday activities.

This book has a number of audiences: first, those with the Verge name that now number in the tens of thousands all over the world; second, the daughters of the Verge ancestry who have married into the other families; third, the many people that visit the Christchurch Priory who will enjoy a story centered around one of its earliest records; fourth, readers that identify with the lives of common folk everywhere, especially their fortitude to take hardships and disappointments and meld them with their faith and accomplishments.

I am hoping that this simple genre of ancestral fiction will prompt many others to bring life to the records that they discover.

PART ONE: CHRISTCHURCH AND THE VERGES

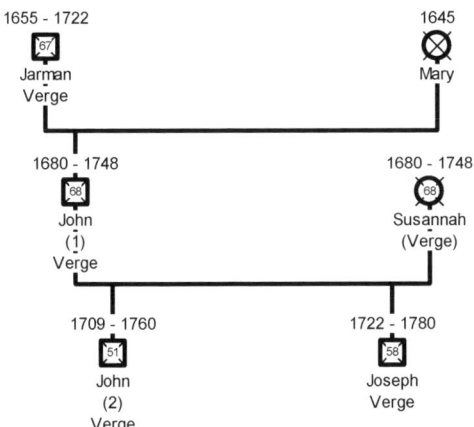

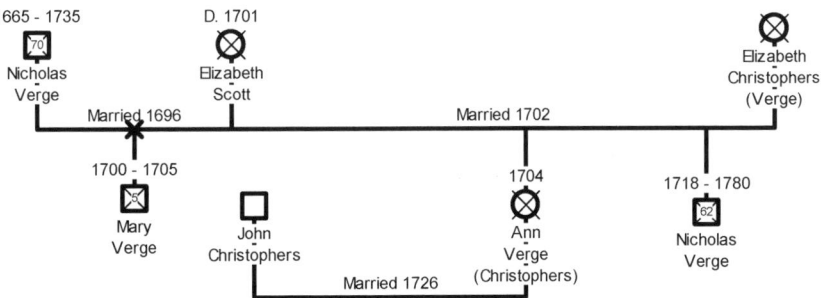

CHAPTER ONE: NICHOLAS AND THE PRIORY

Should you perchance have an opportunity to take a walking tour of Christchurch, England, you will be drawn towards a church of some thousand years that stands just at the edge of the town, commonly known as the Priory. As you walk across the streets that lead to this historic edifice, it will appear as if it is trying to keep an illusionary distance from you, but when you cross the last street and turn towards its entrance, it beckons you to come and enjoy moments of quietness in its rooms and gardens.

If you had taken that walk some three hundred and fifty years ago you would have caught sight of a young lad turning a corner as he made his way towards the Priory. His path took him from his humble home by the sea to his favorite spot near the Priory where he faithfully reflected upon the nature of the world around him, the purpose of his existence and the meaning of his faith. He was a ruddy lad of continental description with a combination of French and German facial features, of normal height, a sober countenance, and a purposeful gait. He dressed the same each day with a long vest over his homemade shirt, and breeches that were just long enough to cover the tops of his socks. On cooler days he took a long waistcoat that served as a blanket to keep out the chill of the wind and the dampness of the fog. His path was repetitive: along the shoreline with its ceaseless lapping waves; onto the bank with its bushes, crags, and flora; up an incline that broadened his view; across a meadow where cows and horses quietly nibbled the damp morning grass; past the ruins of the old castle and across the great Priory walkways. He then turned toward the Isle of Wright, taking the mill run to watch the fish swim in the shallow waters and finally to the Wick ferry where the rivers Stour and Avon meet, a spot that he visited often. Others who came to the same spot distanced themselves from one another without a greeting. They did not come to talk and everyone understood the ritual. On every free day that he had Nicholas made his way to this spot, returning with yet another outlook on his life and times. At other times he took the ferry to Hengistbury, that great expanse of land where walkers could be seen at any time of day looking for some artifact to remind them of life near Christchurch almost two millennia ago. Nicholas was careful in sharing the secret that he found a coin dating back to those times.

Nicholas' parents had settled in a small house near the sea and from there his father carried on a fishery trade. Being ordinary folk, their house was made of a mixture of chalk, clay, straw and timber commonly known as the Tudor style. Nicholas shared a room with his brother, Jarman, who was ten years older than he. At the time that Jarman was old enough to begin school, the only option was St. Michael's Loft which was particularly for gentlemen's sons. Even though the parents were not greatly affluent, they sacrificed beyond measure to provide schooling for their sons. However, both of the brothers had to leave school to help their father provide for the family. This left them longing for more education, the lack of which made them feel somewhat distanced from those things that brought hope, and aspirations. Also, the town itself was limited in offering much to stimulate their desire for more learning.

Their father told them stories of centuries past, how his town began and how it was challenged by war, poverty, religion and isolation. It began with the name of Twynham, meaning the settlement between two rivers. Some one hundred and seventy souls lived there at the time of William the Conqueror, the first Norman King of England. The new King demolished many of the structures that the Saxons had left and began to replace them with his touch. He hastened to ask his servants to build a church near the place where the rivers met. Craftsmen toiled for over a century to complete it and those that remained were rewarded to see such a structure at the center of the town. As Nicholas walked by it each day he looked upon the majestic edifice and projected himself back to that era, experiencing the awe that many others had felt over the centuries.

The grand old Priory was the center of Nicholas' life, as it was for other generations before and after him, and the stories of their lives are incomplete without the knowledge of the Priory's history. The very beginning of its construction is lost in antiquity, but the construction becomes clearer at the beginning of the Norman invasion of England by William of Normandy in the eleventh century. His first task was to send aides all over England to determine how many towns existed, what their populations were, how much wealth they had, what buildings were erected, and how much land was used for each town. The findings were all compiled in a book called The Domesday Book which became the measure of the nation's wealth. King William declared that there should be a place of worship in Christchurch, not similar to the Saxon style, but rather that of Norman construction.

The craftsmen willingly took on the task with great vigor, inspired by the fact that they were bringing the presence of God to their town. The foundation stones for this Priory church were to be laid two miles to the north of the present church. Local people disagreed, wanting the stones laid on the existing Saxon site. However, the powers-that-be overruled the local populace and the stones were taken to St. Catherine's Hill, the new site. The story is told that the very next morning when the workmen returned, they discovered that the stones had been removed and placed on the site of the original Saxon church. The workmen moved the stones back to St. Catherine's Hill, but again, the following morning they found the stones reposing on the Saxon site! This game of cat-and-mouse continued for some time until eventually, the Project Manager, one Ranulf Flambard, decided enough was enough. God had given them a clear message that the building should be constructed on the Saxon site.

Another story that has been passed down is that one day a mysterious carpenter appeared. He neither took his meals with the other men nor was he present when they were paid. A large beam was necessary for the roof and the lumber was measured and carefully cut. It was hoisted to the roof and horror-of-horrors, found to be too short. It had to be lowered back to ground and work ended for the rest of that day. The very next morning when the workmen returned, the beam was missing. It was with feelings akin to awe and amazement that they eventually discovered it in its proper position in the roof and measuring the correct length. The mysterious carpenter never appeared again. They had the answer to their known carpenter by trade. It was Jesus who had helped them to build HIS church! From that day it became known as 'Christ's Church' of Twynham.

The Priory stands above the place where the Avon and Stour meet, a bulwark that draws the townsfolk to its open doors as a place of comfort and refuge. Those who enter the Priory are instantly arrested by the magnificence of its architecture. Even in the entrance itself, the statuette of the pelican feeding her young speaks of the spiritual protection that the church provides. Another step or two and a slight turn to the left opens up a vista of great Norman arches lined up exactly the same on each side of the Nave, reaching some fifty feet to the ceiling as if calling congregants to heights of worship. After the long walk up the aisles, worshippers and visitors alike approach the altar: parents carrying children to be baptized, believers to be confirmed, young lads to assist the Vicars, men and women, young and older to be married, members to be received into the church, the faithful to receive the Eucharist, the needy for healing and all to worship. Beyond the altar is the great choir room where songs are rehearsed for the morning services, evensong, and public concerts, all being accompanied by the resounding music from the majestic pipe organ. At the far end is the Lady's chapel, a sixteenth century addition, constructed for the purpose of smaller group meetings, discussions and other activities.

CHAPTER TWO: BECOMING CITIZENS

It was here that Nicholas lived out his days in cycles of birth, marriage and death with mixtures of joy and sorrow. His father told him stories about what Nicholas' great grandparents had experienced a century or two before his time. During their lifetime the great king Henry VIII ruled England and changed the very heart of every sector of the country. Up until the century of his reign, the Roman Catholic faith was the primary religion of all areas of England. This was changed during the sixteenth century when King Henry VIII broke from the leadership of the pope and introduced a new way of expressing faith in God.

Nicholas' ancestors did not fully understand it all, but many of them adjusted to the emerging Church of England which included segments of the Catholic faith and tenets of the Protestant movement begun by Martin Luther. King Henry VIII intended to destroy all edifices that were part of the Catholic religion, including the Priory in

Christchurch, but this was too much for the townspeople to accept, so along with the last prior, John Draper, they petitioned the king to keep the parish church in perpetuity. On October 23, 1540 the king granted their request which was confirmed on February 12, 1612 by King James I.

On Sundays, along with his parents and older brother, Jarman, Nicholas attended the services at the Priory and felt strengthened for the tasks of the week ahead. As a child, he was baptized in the faith and at the age of thirteen he received his first communion. His whole family was devout and faithfully supported the Church of England. This commitment by Nicholas was one of the foundations of his pilgrimage to Christian maturity. There was evidence of this in his life as he grew into adulthood, committing himself to honesty, uprightness, citizenry, and taking care of the necessities of life.

Young men who grow into early and late adulthood are challenged by many aspects of life such as education, vocation, citizenship, marriage and fulfillment. This was very much the case of Nicholas and Jarman. Nicholas observed how Jarman found his way through the stages of life and was torn between following the example of his older brother and developing a path for himself. Because of the age difference between the two Nicholas had ample time to make his own decisions. Formal schooling reached Christchurch when Jarman was seven years of age, three years before Nicholas was born. By the time that Nicholas entered school, it had become well established in the town, offering lessons in Latin, citizenry, science, mathematics and religion. Nicholas' parents provided the means for him to study these disciplines until the time came when he had to leave school and participate in the fishery with his father and Jarman. Although his formal education ended, he continued with his pursuit of greater knowledge, which became a significant part of his life.

His education was not necessary for his vocation. The fishery business was not his choice but Christchurch offered very little diversity of jobs. Fishing, weaving and brewing were the major means of employment. Fishing thrived along the coastline and was a natural means of livelihood. The primary customers were towns and cities that were situated away from the sea. Weaving did not appeal to Nicholas and his values did not allow him to participate in the brewing trade, so he made himself content with fishing and found satisfaction in the fact that he was contributing to the livelihood of his family. He was well prepared for the time when he would provide for his own wife and children.

Citizenry was very important to Nicholas, a trait that he inherited from his parents. Although the citizens were subject to the king with little rights to pursue social changes, they worked out a life that was pleasing to themselves. A number of factors fostered this way of life. First of all, the majority were deeply conscientious of being upright Christians. Copies of the King James Bible, completed in 1611 had reached his town and there was a copy in his home. It always sat in the same spot, a place that could be readily accessed. Sometimes a family member read and others listened, while at other times members of the family read individually. Bible passages were accepted very literally. The readers followed the biblical instruction that citizens should honor and obey the king, they refrained from those things that were declared as sinful in the Old Testament law, they strictly obeyed the Ten Commandments and faithfully strived to live a consistent Christian life.

Another factor in developing citizenry was the tendency to be social, mannerly, honest, hardworking, and to some extent elitist, especially those that were able to reach a significant level of prosperity. Even though the town was not a highly socio/economic one, the citizens who could afford it could enjoy plays, art, music, politics and overall community improvement. Many of the Shakespearean plays had found their ways to towns and cities all over England. Christchurch, being just a little over one hundred miles from

Stratford-on-Avon, was well familiar with this famous playwright and his works. His plays became a large part of the entertainment for Nicholas and his family.

They cherished peace, not only for their town but for the nation. Many conflicts took place during the time of Nicholas. Just a few years before the birth of Jarman, a great war took place in England between King Charles I and his parliamentarians. Christchurch became one of the centers of the conflict and the parents of the two brothers lived in the midst of it. They related the events to their children when they became old enough to understand what war really meant. Nicholas gasped at the tyranny of the soldiers that used the great Priory as a stable for their horses. He would go there at times to meditate and was stunned at the imprints of their teeth that were left in the pews of the church. Each day on his walk he would look upon the ruins of the Christchurch castle and reflect upon what his hometown must have looked like during the time of war. He did not know that during his lifetime there would yet be more conflicts and tensions.

CHAPTER THREE: THE MARRIAGE OF JARMAN AND MARY

Another factor in the development of adulthood was marriage. As Nicholas reached his teen years, he entertained thoughts of marriage and a family of his own. Jarman married when Nicholas was sixteen. Nicholas watched as Jarman began to befriend some of the ladies in the town and how he became especially friendly with Mary, a very attractive young woman. He remembered the evening when Jarman brought his lady to their home and watched the glances of his parents as they tried to show their acceptance of the young couple. The conversation of the evening was polite but Nicholas discerned a measure of uncertainty by his parents. He detected that Jarman and Mary were realizing this so he quickly began to reverse the uncomfortable atmosphere in the room. By the end of the visit everyone was much more relaxed and comfortable. The experience of the evening left Nicholas thinking deeply about the kind of wife that would please his parents when his time came to marry. This nagging feeling remained with him every time he began to befriend one of the ladies of the town. In the next few years a couple of events took place that impacted his thoughts on marriage. The first was the marriage of Jarman and Mary. Although he was just sixteen years old when this happened, he was mature enough to experience all of the feelings that Jarman was experiencing. He gleaned from his brother the process of preparing for marriage and the responsibilities that go with it. He watched as Mary became more accepted by his family and friends, and his own friendship with her was a token of the closeness that he hoped would develop towards his future wife. He learned more about how to approach a potential future marriage partner, how to lead her to accept him, how to maintain a good relationship, how to build trust in her and how to balance true love with physical desires.

As Jarman and Mary prepared for their marriage one of the first decisions was whether their ceremony would take place in the town office or in a church. A civil wedding was accepted by the society and mostly with little criticism. However, the Priory drew a large congregation every time a wedding took place. The choice of a church wedding became easy for Jarman and Mary. The Christchurch Priory had become a place of refuge for the town. It had survived the war between Henry VIII and the parliamentarians. It lifted the faith of the townspeople. It towered above the Stour and Avon rivers as the guardian of the town and stood as a monument of hope. The couple spoke many times about the reverence of the high altar and looked forward to walking the aisle in such an historic edifice. Both families also anticipated the awe of that moment when the Vicar would read the wedding ceremony.

The time arrived when they publically announced their marriage and set the date to be in the springtime of the next year. A written request was delivered to the Priory asking that it be reserved for their wedding ceremony. The little town of Christchurch looked forward to another time of celebration.

The planning and anticipation meant that they were now spending more time together. The sense of oneness brought a new intimacy between them and their strength was tested more and more as they longed to give themselves to one another. The time finally came when their wills no longer controlled them and Jarman and Mary gave in to their desires.

Both of them were overcome with a myriad of emotions. What was meant for their wedding night was no longer an event to look forward to. A sense of defeat overcame them and they felt there was no reason to remain celibate as they approached the wedding. It did not take long to discover that Mary was pregnant. Pregnancy before marriage was common in the society, with twenty-five per cent of the women being pregnant before marriage. Even though the couple did not feel the shame of the society, they knew that their devout Christian parents would be disappointed, so immediately they hastened to change the date of their marriage so that her pregnancy would not be obvious during the ceremony. The reading of the banns made it difficult to change the dates, which left them with a quick decision. They decided that they would be married in the Priory but not with a public ceremony. They would just go there with witnesses and have the Vicar perform the wedding in private. This crushed Mary's dream of marching down the aisle in the ancient church with loved ones and friends joyously clapping as they walked to the altar. Mary tried to drive it from her mind but she experienced many times of depression as she visualized the event. One day as she walked by the Priory, the door was open and she was drawn to the high altar, where in the silent awe of the moment she experienced the disappointment of it all and blurred the beauty of the altar with her tears.

Nicholas became aware that something was happening about the wedding but he withheld any inquires. Jarman was not as jubilant now as he had been when he talked earlier about it to his brother. He spoke as if Nicholas had discovered their dilemma and finally he related the story to him. Nicholas was not judgmental, but had great compassion for his brother and especially Mary. Their decision gradually became known to the townsfolk and they politely accepted the fact that the wedding would be private. The marriage quietly took place as planned and they settled in their own home looking forward to the birth of their first child.

Nicholas spent many hours dwelling upon what had taken place and processed his emotions. He especially analyzed the impact such an event would have on him as he continued his journey into his late teens and early adulthood. The matter of marriage was not an immediate concern. If he thought of getting married at the same age that Jarman did, he still had almost ten years before he would get serious about choosing a wife. He walked many times to his place of solitude and dwelt upon his future.

CHAPTER FOUR: THE CHILDREN OF JARMAN AND MARY

The life of Nicholas did not unfold by just a series of decisions but rather by his openness to the changing times in the town of Christchurch and area. One of these was a major development in the expression of the Christian faith. While the Church of England was very prominent, there were other groups emerging that wanted to go further in representing the New Testament Church. One of these groups was the Puritans whose beginning went back to the sixteenth century at the time that Henry VIII broke from the Catholic Church. Some who became part of the Church of England did not believe that Henry and the church leaders went far enough in following the faith of the New Testament so they began to preach the biblical truths that were neglected. One such person was John Bunyan who had a deep spiritual conversion and passionately began to tell his story. His heart was stirred by a sermon from the Song of Solomon that planted the words "my love, my dove" in his heart.

These words followed him until he gave himself fully to the faith and left a legacy of preaching and writing. His greatest written accomplishment was, "The Pilgrims Progress" written in 1678. Nicholas was just thirteen when the book was written and later in his late teens he was able to read it. The book awakened spiritual longings that he felt were not being satisfied in the ritual of church services. Although he had great respect for those who faithfully ministered to the Christchurch congregation, he felt that something more was needed. Nicholas began to search the family Bible in more detail and joined some of the Christian groups that were being established at that time. He did not neglect the services of the Priory, but looked to the Puritan groups for his spiritual development. This change impacted every aspect of his life and especially in the way that he would approach marriage.

Nicholas did not pursue formal education but he kept up with the changing society and stayed in touch with world affairs as much as was possible.

He took an interest in the local government and had many audiences with the mayor on the betterment of the little town. His other activities included his participation in the game of cricket which had become popular in the seventeenth century. He also developed a love for the arts. During the time that Nicholas was maturing to adulthood a number of events took place that were very close to him.

Among these were the births of the children of Jarman and Mary, all three of whom were born before Nicholas married. The first child was born just after Nicholas was sixteen which all at once made him feel much more mature. Being an uncle brought a measure of responsibility to participate in the growth of the child. Nicholas felt his inadequacy, but the closeness to his little nephew made up for all of the other feelings. Jarman and Mary were ecstatic about their son and named him John, a common name in the country and also prominent in the Bible. The morning of his christening was sunny but cool. Their walk to the

Priory was brisk and with a certain amount of pageantry. As the grandparents, parents and Nicholas walked in step to the grand old Priory, Mary recalled the shadow over the joy of her wedding, but now she was aglow at the baptism of her child. Many of her friends were there to share in her joy and to express their love and support. Baby John was the center of it all.

Nicholas would now be able to observe the raising of his nephew, little John, as he developed through the many stages of growth, and also to observe the impact upon the parents. His first observation was that Jarman and Mary spent just a few months alone before John was born, leaving them little time to adjust to one another and with little resources to fully prepare a home for their family. The strain to provide for a child and at the same time finish their home was a heavy burden for them, especially in a town of limited opportunities. They willingly accepted the fact that they would have to live on meagre provisions in order to give John all that they felt he should have.

Nicholas drew a number of conclusions from their situation. One was that the love for a child could inadvertently challenge their love for one another. At times, Mary felt a measure of neglect when Jarman spent their resources not only on necessities but on playthings for John. Jarman also felt neglect when Mary had to give so much time to John, feeling at times that they had skipped that stage where newly married couples lived footloose and free.

There were happy exchanges though, as John endeared himself to them with all of his inquisitiveness and allowable mischief. The number of stories that Nicholas heard about the happiness that John gave them far outweighed complaints of neglect. Nicholas could not believe that simple children events could become such ecstatic parent events. Mary hastily proclaimed the news of the first smile, the first grip, the unceasing babble, mobile knees, vertical moments, first steps, first real word, and then that busy stage of exploration. It did not take long for the family to become "three of us" instead of "two parents and one child".

Nicholas observed all of this and became very positive about marriage and family, hoping that nothing would occur to blur that outlook. Two years later a second son was born to Jarman and Mary. At first there was a repeat of the jubilation of their first child, but soon they began to notice that their newborn son, William, was experiencing health difficulties that left them greatly worried. Infant mortality was widespread all around them and in places beyond. Even with the best efforts of the parents, they could not control the innumerable diseases and accidents which plagued them. Some thirty per cent of the children died before they were fifteen. At the time of Nicholas' birth the plague was taking its toll all over England. There was not a sudden end to the disease and remnants of it still lingered in a number of towns, including Christchurch. The symptoms of the plague were somewhat similar to other diseases such as measles, whooping cough and smallpox, so with very few professionals in the town, it was difficult to identify little William's sickness. They worked tirelessly to keep the fever down and to strengthen his body against other attacks. At times they thought he was getting better, only to have their hopes crushed again. Just toward the end of the second month of his illness, William could no longer fight the enemy diseases, and he died in Mary's arms. When Nicholas reached their house, both Jarman and Mary were in despair at the loss of their treasure. In the midst of all of the sorrow, there were things to be done, so Nicholas, seeing the distress of the couple, and following the custom of their time went about draping the windows, preparing mourning bands and taking the news to the Priory. Within minutes the bell tolled three times indicating that another child less than one year old had died.

The death of William was a shock to Nicholas, abruptly interrupting his pleasure of observing John's growth over the first two years of his life. He was overwhelmed with all that had transpired and made his way to that place of refuge and reflection that he had visited many times before. He returned there more often now as he advanced toward his twentieth year and beyond. It bothered him that the town didn't seem to very concerned with trying to overcome the diseases that took so many children, so the tolling of the bell did not cease. Nicholas felt the risk of bringing children into a society that was not prepared to protect them from unknown diseases and he was also distressed by the perils of the birthing of children by untrained midwives. He determined that marriage and children for him would be postponed until there was a safer environment for mothers and children. He thought much about the status of women in the society of his time. Very few women were allowed to participate in matters pertaining to politics, social justice, employment opportunities or even their own education. Because of his private study and his participation in improving the society, his thoughts on these things were quite different from many of the other citizens.

CHAPTER FIVE: THE MYSTERY OF THE BOYS' PARENTS

Nicholas also felt a subtle mystery concerning his parents. Although they told their sons about events that happened in the past, they told them very little about themselves. As Nicholas grew older he kept wondering why he and Jarman had names that were not common in England. As he became more in touch with European news and other writings, he observed these names were much more common there and his parents seemed to identify with them. This raised many questions as to his ancestry and he wondered if his parents were even born in England. If so, was there some reason why they did not want to talk about that part of their lives? Did they come to Christchurch before they were old enough to remember? Did both of them come at different times and meet somewhere in the vicinity? Were they among those who escaped the persecution of Christian believers in France and felt threatened to make it known? Were there other Verges living in the region that their parents knew about and were connected with? If so, did their parents have a falling out with these Verges and not talk to him and Jarman about them? Many times these questions whirled around in Nicholas' mind as he visited his spot between the rivers, and over time based upon the knowledge of the times, he created a scenario that helped to depict what may have happened in the lives of his parents.

He decided that whether they came from France directly to Christchurch or by way of other towns such as Poole and Swanage, it was quite possible that they or their ancestors were part of a protestant group, the Huguenots, who sought freedom of religion in England during the 17th century. These were devout Christian believers and their expression of Christianity was far different from the Roman Catholic Church at that time. They were one of the many groups that were impacted by the protestant reformation of Martin Luther in the sixteenth century. Cardinal Richelieu in France persecuted these Huguenots right up to the time of his death just twelve years before Jarman was born. Maybe his parents left France around that date. The emigration of the Huguenots from France continued after Richelieu died and even up to the eighteenth century. Those seeking refuge from Catholic domination in France could now find freedom in the cities and towns of England. Their journey to England was probably the same as that of hundreds more who escaped religious persecution in France. They were devout Christians who suffered under Richelieu and longed for freedom to express their faith. They undoubtedly lived in southern France because of its proximity to the venue of the reformation. Their pilgrimage from France to Southern England was probably towards the north, dodging those that pursued them. They leaned upon the faith of their fathers who made the same journey a century earlier when the Huguenot persecution was at its height. Along the way they took refuge in the homes of the faithful and many of them joined them on their journey. The uncertainty of reaching the goal of their pilgrimage was heavy upon them, but the burden lifted as they came close to the channel that separated them from the land of England and freedom. Just as the Israelites viewed the Promised Land across the Jordan River, so did this little group of pilgrims strain their eyes to see the cliffs of Dover or the port of Southampton and other entry points of England.

The ship in which they sailed could have been the cutter, made by Huguenots who were ready to take them across the channel. The crossing to England was not very long so the journey was probably without event. Upon seeing the shores of Britain, the group might have found a secluded place in the ship to have a thanksgiving prayer service, after which they disembarked to a new life. The more that Nicholas dwelt upon this scenario, the more he came to believe it.

CHAPTER SIX: NICHOLAS' FIRST MARRIAGE

The years of Nicholas' twenties developed into a routine of work, church, community involvement and family. During that time Mary and Jarman were ecstatic to welcome their third child, a girl whom they named Charity. She was born seven years after the death of William. Nicholas now had a nephew and a niece as part of his life which made him think again upon marriage and family. He realized that life is made up of sadness as well as joy and as he approached his thirtieth year he became serious about marriage and children.

He was aware that it was acceptable for women to be married at twelve years of age with the parents' consent, so it was not easy to find ladies still unmarried after their teen years. He hoped for a partner as close as possible to his age, but the norms of the society made that difficult. There were some ladies, however, that had not received consent from their parents, mostly because they did not approve of their daughter's suitor and

Nicholas knew about one or two of these, especially one that he saw many times walking to and from the Priory. Because of his intention to postpone his marriage, he had not attempted to make acquaintance, but he had inadvertently found himself noticing her. Most of the time she was wearing the new English dress style known as Mantua that had reached Christchurch a couple of years earlier. It was a one piece dress hanging from the shoulders to the floor with a high square neckline that was more modest than the broad shoulder to shoulder neckline. Her hair hung in long curls stacked high over her forehead. She walked with her back straight and with an intentional step as if she were determined to reach her destination on time. Her countenance was fair and portrayed much confidence. Nicholas felt that she looked his way during the last few times that they passed by one another. He determined that he was going to make conversation the next time that they met. And he did. It happened as they made their way out of the Priory after evensong. The air was warm and the evening rays of the sun cast shadows across the courtyard. Those leaving for home slowed their pace as if to prolong a few more moments of peace and solitude. Nicholas took the lead in beginning a conversation about the reluctance of the worshippers to hasten their journey homeward. The young woman quickly returned the sentiment and went on to express her feelings about the way everyone was sharing the peacefulness of the moment. The dialogue flowed easily as they found themselves walking together and slowing down as they approached the parting place just outside the gate. Nicholas was bold as he told her his name and welcomed hers. There was a certain pounding in his heart as he heard her voice gently saying, "Elizabeth".

They detoured from their usual path and chose one that would lengthen their conversation and also bring them to a place of rest on the banks of the Avon. There the conversation led to a personal level as they shared the stories of their upbringing, their outlook on the society, their setbacks and goals, and cautiously about singleness and marriage. Just before parting, they planned a walk together to the spot that Nicholas had visited many times. Their walks and talks brought them closer together until the moment arrived when Nicholas decided to propose marriage. However, immediately after he made that decision, he was confronted with a series of doubts and uncertainties. The thought of giving up his goal of higher learning distressed him to the point that he became very indecisive about marriage. His intention of attending the university at Oxford which was not far from Christchurch, lingered with him throughout his twenties as he struggled to find the means to enrol. Even though he had accumulated some funds in the last two years, it would take two more years to have sufficient money to make his dream materialize. He dreamed often of Oxford: walking its halls of knowledge, engrossing himself in the volumes so neatly lined upon its shelves, listening to the wisdom of its faculty, and most of all walking the stage of its grand hall to receive the reward of his studies. He also dreamed of becoming a husband and father, establishing a home, watching his children make their first steps and hearing their first word, making sure that they received good schooling and watching them walk the stage to receive the honour of their education. Accepting the fact that it would have to be him or his children who would reach that stage of higher learning, he decided to defer these accomplishments to his children, and just a few days later he proposed to Elizabeth who quickly accepted.

Nicholas and Elizabeth, being much older than the norm, did not have to receive parental consent. The parents on both sides were delighted and accepted the marriage without hesitation. Nicholas and Elizabeth looked back at the events surrounding the marriage of Jarman and Mary and made a firm vow that they would not make the same mistake. They enthusiastically looked forward to the walk down the aisle of the Priory and the offering of their vows in the sight of family and friends.

They broke with the tradition of a fall wedding and set the date for a summer one instead. It seemed as even nature prepared itself for the wedding. The sun had warmed the morning, leaving no room for the fog that usually settled upon Christchurch and vicinity. As was the custom, the wedding would be between early morning and noon. Nicholas and Elizabeth prepared themselves at their homes and the bride had the privilege of being escorted to the church in one of the first coaches found in Christchurch. As she rode, she remembered the stories about the great Queen Elizabeth who gloriously ruled England for the last half of the sixteenth century. Her name had spread all over the world and became identified with the many positive changes that took place in her country. As she was making her way to the church, Elizabeth imagined the pomp of that great queen who had visited Christchurch a century before. Nicholas had prepared himself for the moment to receive her as she walked the aisle in the magnificent Priory church. He was entering the third decade of his life and Elizabeth was past twenty, thus they had become very well known in the whole community, not only for their familiarity, but because of their involvement in the society. Consequently the nave was filled with family, personal friends, common group members, parishioners, community leaders and those who looked upon themselves as being mentored by Nicholas.

Nicholas took his place at the altar and watched as his bride walked the aisle to begin their life together. Applause filled the nave as Elizabeth began her procession towards the one who would be her partner for life. She was radiantly dressed in a long flowing blue gown accented with other colours, indicating that she was not just one of the common folk of the town, but fairly prestigious. The ceremony was made up of prayers, chants, music, vows, and the giving of rings. The Vicar pronounced them husband and wife and authorized the verger to write in the record book: Nicholas Verge and Elizabeth Scott married July 16, 1696.

Dancing, feasting and blessings from family and friends followed as they celebrated well into the day and then the very happy couple walked to the modest Tudor house that Nicholas had built for them.

CHAPTER SEVEN: JOY AND SORROW

Nicholas was a loving husband and looked forward to the time when children would bring joy to their home. The wait was not long. Elizabeth carried her baby throughout the fall and winter with much anticipation, but as springtime drew near, she became aware that things were not going well. Medical attention was not readily available and this being her first child she had little understanding of what was happening. Many times, Nicholas would feel the movements of the child but he became worried when they became weaker. With two months left before the birth should take place, Elizabeth consulted midwives about her physical condition and her worries. There were different opinions, and most of them advised her to be prepared for a stillbirth. They informed Elizabeth that stillbirths happened most often between the twenty-fourth and twenty-eighth week of pregnancy. Early in March, Elizabeth called for a midwife to remain with her throughout the ordeal ahead of her. A week later a stillborn daughter was born to Nicholas and Elizabeth. Although there was no requirement to register the death, they named her Joanne.

Recovery from the sad event came slowly to Nicholas and Elizabeth. Mothers and fathers and church leaders advised them to accept the death as an act of God's sovereignty, but although they politely accepted the advice, they felt that some responsibility rested upon the slow improvement of health standards in the town. They now faced a difficult decision as to whether they should delay more children until things got much better. During the next two years they made every effort possible to bring the matter to the attention of the doctors, nurses and midwives, but nothing significant happened. They lived between the anticipation of having another child and the fear of the consequences. Jarman and Mary spoke many times with them about their own fear of having other children after William died and the long delay before the birth of Charity. John, the first child of Jarman was now seventeen and Charity was six.

Many devout believers throughout England felt strongly that the conception of children should not be prevented in any way. The two couples included this in their conversations, sometimes disagreeing with one another and at other times sharing in the same state of uncertainty. After two years of such discussions, Nicholas and Elizabeth decided to have another child.

Her pregnancy was filled with doubts and fears, but also with hope. They both rested in the fact that God was able to bring them through this event. It was a time of anxiety for Elizabeth, but she became more encouraged as each day unfolded without any difficulties. Three years had passed since Joanne was born, and now as the eighteenth century dawned upon Christchurch, a baby girl was born to Nicholas and Elizabeth. They hastened to the Priory to have her baptised and given the name Mary.

The family settled into a happy routine of work, family events, entertainment, church activities, and times of delight as Mary said her first word, walked her first step, and continually amused her parents with unexpected behavior. Over the past few years Nicholas had moved beyond just fishing to becoming a fish merchant. This added a greater responsibility to making a living for his family, but it also provided times throughout the day when he could spend time at home with Elizabeth and Mary. He was now in his mid-thirties and life could not be better. The sadness of losing Joanne slowly faded away and was replaced by the joy of having a beautiful and very active daughter.

Nicholas and Elizabeth had no way of knowing what lay ahead for the next two years so they celebrated every new event in Mary's life and gave themselves to the child to raise her with the same standards by which they had been raised. It was well into the second year after Mary's birth that Elizabeth began to feel a sense of overall discomfort in her body. Fevers became frequent and headaches lingered for days. She tried to fight the malaise, but despite all efforts it worsened to the point where vomiting became common.

Nicholas began to notice the change in her and together they tried to get to the root of her condition. He began to read everything that he could find pertaining to health, and discussed Elizabeth's ailment with those whom he thought might have some knowledge of her condition. Many felt that it might be smallpox but it could not be verified until a rash appeared. The harsh reality was not long coming when rashes began to appear on Elizabeth's face. Nicholas was not just faced with accepting his wife's impending death, but also with preventing the spread of the disease to himself and Mary. If it were just him he would gladly hold Elizabeth in his arms and comfort her even at the risk of death, but she insisted that he do everything that he could to save himself and Mary.

The next few days were filled with pure agony for all three. It was impossible to explain to little Mary why she could not touch her mother and that her daddy could not either. The two weeks felt like a lifetime as the three of them expressed their frustration of not being able to live as they always did. When Mary slept, Nicholas and Elizabeth talked long into the night knowing that the moment of death could arrive at any time. They took advantage of these moments to reflect on the happiness of the past two years and their plans for their Mary whom they enjoyed together for such a short time. Nicholas made promises that Mary would be raised according to the vows that they had made about her future. She would be schooled even at the point of sacrifice and taught according to the values of their faith. Realizing the challenge for Nicholas to raise a child on his own, Elizabeth encouraged him to not delay a second marriage. They humoured one another that he might find another Elizabeth to carry on the likeness of his present family.

The moment that he dreaded came sooner than expected. Nicholas had been sleeping in Elizabeth's room on a small cot. He tossed to and fro throughout the nights wanting to be awake when the time came. On the day of her passing, he awoke just as the first rays of the sun filtered through the curtains. The strange quietness spoke loudly to him and he knew without looking that Elizabeth had passed into another realm where diseases could not plague her any more. The funeral was swift as two days later she was placed to rest in the churchyard of the old Priory.

CHAPTER EIGHT: NICHOLAS' SECOND MARRIAGE

Emotions engulfed Nicholas as he returned to the routine of life, but he also faced the realities that Elizabeth had talked about many times. He experienced a great sense of betrayal to Elizabeth when he thought of marriage, especially when he felt that he should hasten another marriage for the sake of Mary. He was also worried whether a new relationship just for practical purposes would be genuine. He decided to let his mind rest from such things for a season and do all that he could for Mary.

Being a single father with a daughter too young for schooling was a challenge for Nicholas. It was normal for families to have servants, but because they had only Mary, Elizabeth and Nicholas had decided to put away the money for Mary's schooling, rather than pay a servant. Now that Elizabeth was gone, Nicholas faced two pressures, one of paying for a servant and the other hoping that Mary would adjust to a replacement for her mother. Leaving the house in the morning weighed heavily upon him. His first day away was his most difficult as he lingered at the door, but Mary was the stronger of the two and didn't seem to mind staying with her nanny.

It wasn't long before he realized that Mary needed a mother so he began to befriend a few ladies who would relate to his personality and lifestyle. He did not seek "falling in love" as much as he sought a wife who would love his daughter. Nicholas talked many times to his friend, William Christophers, about his situation and found the conversations very helpful. William, who married just a year before Nicholas did, identified with him especially in the losing of a child. However, both of them were now compensated by having children who were very much alive and active. William talked at times about his sister and how marriage seemed to elude her every time that she found someone of interest. Their conversations about William's sister came up more often and finally

William decided to bring Nicholas and his sister together. The Priory was the meeting place of the town, a place where conversations took place as parishioners walked to and from worship. It was here on a chilly Sunday morning that William manipulated a meeting of Nicholas and Elizabeth. As William chatted with his sister after the morning service he pointed out Nicholas and little Mary on their way out of the courtyard and walked toward them. It wasn't long before all three were sharing accolades about Mary's lofty stance and her politeness of speech. She happily took hold of the outstretched hand of Elizabeth and enjoyed a walk about the courtyard, feeling something akin to the walks with her mother. Elizabeth took her eyes off Mary a few times to take a glance at Nicholas and wished the day was longer.

Both of them made efforts to "accidently" meet again. However, they did not have to arrange it that way, for they met unplanned at the market. Mary spotted Elizabeth and was quick to tell her father that she was there. Mary took her father by his hand and led him to Elizabeth, creating a bond that was not yet complete but very much in the making. After a lengthy conversation and some prompting from Mary, plans were made to meet again at the home of Nicholas.

The times together increased and both realized that marriage was their destiny. Nicholas reflected upon how he and his former wife had jokingly suggested that maybe there would be another Elizabeth to become part of the family, a thought that was becoming a reality. The couple began to talk seriously about marriage, not just out of convenience, but because of a bond that had grown between them, along with a close mother-daughter relationship between Elizabeth and Mary. These were confirmations of their plans, so on one of their walks along the Priory walkway without any formal proposal, they decided that they would marry. The news was happily received by Elizabeth's brother, William Christophers, their relatives and many friends.

Nicholas had experienced the joy of his first wedding in the Priory, and also the sadness of the burial of a child and wife there. Both he and Elizabeth wondered how they would feel if their wedding was held in the same place as before. Would memories of Nicholas' first love return? Would Elizabeth be wondering if he was thinking more of his first wedding? Would he be overcome with repeated emotions of joy and sadness? These were just some of the questions that they tried to answer as they tested the limits of the honesty of each other. Elizabeth decided to share a secret that might help to finalize their decision. Not knowing how Nicholas would react, she told him that she was among those who attended his first wedding. She went on to say that as she watched the ceremony she was happy for his bride, but for a fleeting moment she thought how happy she would be if she were the other Elizabeth. Nicholas detected the warmth of her words and understood. Without any further discussions, they decided that the wedding would take place in the Priory. Mary was elated to know that Elizabeth would be her new mother.

Even though Elizabeth quickly agreed to the marriage and looked forward to her new life with Nicholas and Mary, she was processing many valid questions. Was Nicholas marrying her just to be a mother for Mary? Did he feel the same love for her as he felt for his first wife? Could she live up to her standards? Would the same easy relationship with Mary continue? Elizabeth felt it strange that she would think upon the marriages of King Henry VIII some hundred years before her. Even though he was instrumental in bringing about many positive changes in England, and establishing a new way of life and religion, he did not have a good record of matrimonial affairs. Although he was married to Queen Katherine, he was enamoured by Mary Boleyn and made her his mistress, not only because of his love for her but because his association with her gave him a more cosmopolitan image. Elizabeth wondered if Nicholas would become like Henry and cast her off for someone else, especially if she could not give him an heir. The way in which Henry left Mary Boleyn and chose her sister, Anne, reminded Elizabeth how fickle marriage could be. The story of King Henry VIII and the way in which he manipulated the beheading of Anne was just too much for her to dwell upon. She hastened to turn her thoughts to her wedding and began to prepare for the upcoming event.

At all times the Priory is a place of beauty, but when it is prepared for a marriage it is inexplicitly charming. Its hues blend in such a way that visitors seem to visually traverse the whole interior lest some speck of its splendour be overlooked. Brides must be aware that the audience could be lost in the grandeur of the Priory rather than in the beauty of the bride. Elizabeth was aware of this but she did not feel jealous for she too had the same love for the Priory and felt honoured to share that love with all that came. She was also aware that this was a second marriage for Nicholas, but neither of them wanted `second` to be a factor in the ceremony. This was a first for Elizabeth so Nicholas was adamant they should spare no expense for her wedding attire and that Mary would be one of her attendants. The marriage was to be a message to those present that they were bonded together with love, and that this ceremony would portray that. The dazzling gown, the precise steps, the smiles of the wedding party, the applause of the crowd, and the overall joy of the occasion confirmed the sincerity of what was taking place. The Vicar pronounced them man and wife and the verger added another marriage record into the Priory record book. They settled in the house that Nicholas had built some years earlier. The marriage of Elizabeth and Nicholas grew stronger and so did the bond between Mary and Elizabeth.

CHAPTER NINE: ELIZABETH AND MARY

The family of Verges now consisted of the parents of Nicholas and Jarman; Nicholas and Elizabeth with their child Mary; and Jarman and Mary, with their children, John and Charity. There were birthday celebrations, Christmas dinners, play times and the attending of events that took place in their town of Christchurch. There were visits from home to home and picnics by the rivers of Stour and Avon. Many times they sat together at the Priory during the Sunday morning services, creating a bond within the family. Charity wished that she could be an altar server as John had been but such opportunities were not open to young ladies. Schooling became more available and improvements were made in the health services even though they were still a long way from what was needed. Life is made up of segments of experiences, joyful ones that are cherished forever and difficult ones that are wished away. The family routine of life became predictable but within the next few years there would be unexpected and unwanted occurrences. The first of these was the passing of the parents of Nicholas and Jarman. They reached the sixth decade of their lives which was beyond the average life expectancy at that time. However, their years of toil, their struggle to provide for their sons, their times of sorrow at the loss of their grandchildren and the many bouts of sickness over the years left them frail. They subtly conveyed signals to the children and grandchildren that time was fast ebbing out for them. Within the same year they both passed away and were spared the sorrow of events to come. They were laid to rest in the Priory churchyard.

The passing of the parents of Nicholas and Jarman created a measure of tension within the two families. In this era inheritances were distributed according to the procedure of countries or regions. In some jurisdictions the bequest was left to the oldest son, in others it was shared amongst the family, but seldom did the daughters receive anything of value. The parents of Nicholas and Jarman did not leave a will so the inheritance had to be determined by the system in place at that time. However, this meant that each family did not receive an equal portion, simply because Nicholas did not have a son. Watching Jarman receiving twice as much of the bequest as he did, left him with disappointment that Jarman did not share with Mary. Elizabeth coached him through the process, doing all that she could to maintain good relationships between the families. After all, they had Mary and time was on their side for more children. She humoured Nicholas that maybe there would be many sons to receive their inheritance, but they would break with the system and include the daughters as well.

Although Nicholas and Elizabeth enjoyed Mary and loved her very much they did look forward to having a child together. Just after one year of marriage Elizabeth discovered that she was pregnant and looked forward to the birth with both joy and a measure of anxiety. Jarman's wife, Mary, talked to her many times about William who died in his first year and how his death left her with times of great depression. Elizabeth listened compassionately, sometimes projecting Mary's thoughts to her situation as her pregnancy advanced. She also listened to Nicholas as he recounted the stillbirth of Joanne. As the days went by, she dismissed the anxiety of these events and prepared herself to welcome another child to be a sister or brother to Mary. She was devoted to the care of Mary, and remained a mother to her even as the time drew near for the addition of her own child to the family.

Mary had just entered her fourth year when Elizabeth's new baby arrived. After the midwife presented the newborn girl to Elizabeth and Nicholas, she was introduced to Mary. The moment was short but the intensity of the union was beyond expectation. After settling on the name Ann, Nicholas, Elizabeth and Mary took her to the Priory to be baptized and the bonded family was complete. This was certainly one of those times to cherish forever, but many times in the midst of joy, sorrow lurks behind the scenes. Thus was the plight of this family as in the midst of their jubilation there was an invisible event lurking that would quickly become visible.

The visibility first appeared in the form of spots on Mary's body, spots that would not go away. Elizabeth monitored them with hope but also with moments of hopelessness. Her first step was to keep Ann away from Mary, a task that crushed both of them, especially Mary who could vaguely remember a similar experience when her mother was very ill. How could Ann, a child in her first year, understand why she could not be cuddled anymore, and how can a child of four forfeit those moments of surrogate motherhood? To Nicholas and Elizabeth it was a cruelty that had no resolution. They steeled themselves from the blast of anguish as much as possible in order to offer Mary the comfort and encouragement that she needed. Nicholas relived the anguish of the moment when he discovered that his first wife was stricken with a malady that would take her from him. He recalled how he kept Mary away from her dying mother, and now the circumstances were reversed, drawing him into an immeasurable sense of sorrow that he tried to hide from his wife and children. He had looked forward to a bright future for Mary with times of joy that his first wife would have experienced if she were living. Nicholas had entertained the thought that maybe she would look down on the events with great pleasure. But this was not to be. He tried to banish the reality of what was happening, but underneath he knew that no alternative was in sight. He repeated the dissatisfaction with the health services in Christchurch but even with the improvements over his lifetime, the town still lacked in medical services and especially in overcoming diseases.

Days wore on as little Mary became weaker. Jarman's wife, Mary, looked back to the death of her son William and tried to console Nicholas and Elizabeth. Other members of the Verge family and many friends surrounded the couple with support and love. Every Sunday in the Priory Mary's name was mentioned by the Vicar as he presented prayers for those who were sick. News of her sickness spread throughout the town; some experienced similar sorrow, while others had hardened to the constant tolling of the Priory bell.

Mary's strength weakened, her face paled, and her hands could no longer reach out to greet. One dulcet evening as Elizabeth was preparing a liquid meal for her, Mary drifted into her final sleep. News quickly reached the Priory and its bell tolled seven times announcing to the town that another child of four years had passed away. Two days later she was laid to rest next to her mother in the Priory churchyard.

CHAPTER TEN: BEYOND CHRISTCHURCH

Nicholas, who had lost his firstborn daughter, Joanne, was now faced with the reality of the death of his second daughter, Mary, and was left with little Ann as his only child. The loss of a wife and two children in the eight years since his first marriage left him with emptiness, agony, and tinges of bitterness. The love of Elizabeth and Ann sustained him in this time of brokenness, and he in turn upheld them as they journeyed through this time of sorrow.

In the midst of this difficult time there came a moment of joy into the Verge family in the event of the wedding of Jarman's son, John. For a couple of years he had been building a relationship with Susannah Moores, a young lady who had grown up in Christchurch, attended the same school as John and was part of the congregation of the Priory. John was happy to know that although his grandparents had died before the marriage would take place they knew Susannah and was pleased that John had chosen her to be his wife. Nicholas, who had reconciled with his brother, became involved in the preparations of the wedding and stood as an official witness to it. As with Nicholas and his first wife, Elizabeth, John and Susannah, were married in the nave of the Priory, providing room for all of their friends to attend.

Nicholas, Elizabeth and their adorable Ann developed a bond born out of the distress of death and the exuberance of life. Life overcame death and their home became a place of liveliness, love, humour, entertainment, and peace. Elizabeth developed into an exemplary mother to her child and a mentor to younger mothers who needed help in raising their children. Nicholas immersed himself in expanding his fishing business which raised their standard of living enough for them to participate more in the recreational events of Christchurch. One of their favourites was the "coffee shop" culture that originated in London and had expanded to towns all around the country. The shops became a place for social conversation, business deals, political debates, planning events and displaying affluence. Charity, now fourteen, took care of her cousin, Ann, while Nicholas and Elizabeth enjoyed times at the shops with their friends.

Nicholas and Elizabeth also enjoyed the theatre. Nicholas had been interested in Shakespeare since his youth, following the many changes in the way Shakespeare's plays were presented. Such presentations were not always as sophisticated in Christchurch compared to the London plays, and neither were the bona fide theatres for their presentations, but they improvised. The town folks thoroughly enjoyed the plays, especially if one of the locals acted the role of one of the characters. Jarman and Nicholas worked hard to have the means to seat Mary and Elizabeth in prominent places in the theatre and with great pride they did so on occasion.

The Priory was still the center of the life for the two families. Nicholas and Jarman and their wives were faithful to the worship services, especially when John, who was now in his twenty-third year, read the Scriptures at evensong. He had been confirmed many years earlier, not just as a ritual but as an act of faith and dedication to service for God. While the age for confirmation could be as early as ten Charity had postponed it until she was fourteen. Nicholas and Elizabeth looked forward to the time when their little Ann would join many of her friends in the events taking place at the Priory. They also looked forward to maybe having a son who would be one of the altar boys, a task for which Ann would never be accepted because of her gender.

Elizabeth was happy with her life but was puzzled by a nagging sense of discontent. Although she was delighted with the thought of more children, she felt a measure of being trapped as she settled into being a homemaker. The daily routine of predictable events eventually led to monotony and many times her mind drifted to the glamour of cities.

Transportation by coach increased significantly during the seventeenth century and had reached into cities beyond London. Over time the stark coaches became more sophisticated in style and comfort, which made them not just carriers for business or necessary travel, but for pleasure as well

Elizabeth had longed for such a journey and after some persuasion upon Nicholas, they sacrificed some of their resources to make it happen. Visiting London was more than they could afford so they settled for the town of Southampton. They could have travelled by boat, but their wish was to see the countryside and to visit towns along the way. Even their little town of Christchurch appeared quite different from the raised view of the carriage. They traversed the main street, taking them past the Priory with all its sad and happy memories, then along the river Stour and the spot where Nicholas came so often, and later they watched as the town become smaller and disappeared altogether. They passed through other towns as they continued their journey, each with its unique features offering the couple interesting shops, delightful tea rooms, spontaneous friendships, walks through the villages, and restful inns. They reached Southampton, a bustling town much larger than the city of Christchurch. The couple was fascinated by the number of cafes and inns and took some time to find a place that had a tinge of luxury, but still within their budget. They chose an inn away from the busy trading ships, but close enough to the shoreline to hear the waves as they did at home. They spoke many times about Ann back in Christchurch with her aunt and uncle and wondered if she were lonely and wishing she could be with her parents. Being away from home was new to them and sometimes it brought feelings of guilt, not just because of leaving Ann, but because they were spending money upon themselves. This was something different from their way of living, a test of spending beyond necessity, and an attempt to legitimatize a departure from the mundane. It was also an attempt to introduce a trend to Ann that time for each other builds a stronger family.

CHAPTER ELEVEN: THE DEATH OF SARAH

Nicholas and Elizabeth cherished their young daughter and were thankful that she remained so healthy and happy. The thought of more brothers and sisters for Ann was always something that they looked forward to with a mixture of anxiety and anticipation. Two years after the birth of Ann, Elizabeth announced to Nicholas that another child was on the way. The birth of the little girl, Sarah, was without any complications which increased the joy of the couple and especially made little Ann very happy. Each event in the life of Sarah brought back memories of Mary, some with jubilation and some with anxiety, but in the midst of all the setbacks, surprises, and difficult times, the family settled into the pleasantries of living.

Ann and Sarah entertained one another, protected one another, comforted one another and grew together with excellent health. For the next three years there were just the two of them to liven up their home and to erase memories that had filled the parents' hearts with fear. New memories were created that took the place of sad ones, singing replaced mourning, happiness restored hope, love abounded, laughing overcame crying with the exception of Sarah's determination to get things that belonged to herself and others. Nicholas and Elizabeth overwhelmingly enjoyed both of the girls. This was a time for living, for reading stories around the fire, walks along the beach, summer picnics, games for tots and parents together, dinners with family and friends, Sunday walks to the Priory, Christmases, Easter bonnets and much more. Nicholas walked many times to his meditation place, not to reflect on the difficulties of life but to experience gratitude for all that was taking place in his home.

When Ann became six years old and Sarah three, more joy was added to their home when the first boy was born into the family. Elizabeth was filled with thankfulness that all went well with the birth and even more thankful when she presented Nicholas with his first son. He was overwhelmed with joy as he held the boy in his arms, not replacing the bliss of holding his daughters, but acknowledging the far reaching implications of having a son. He would now have an heir to take his place in the family and to carry on the generations of Verges. Even though he was younger than Ann and Sarah, in keeping with the society, he would be their protector and advisor. He was baptized in the Priory and named John, a simple name but with meaning, especially as it relates to the disciple of Jesus.

For eight years there was no death in the family which was long enough to accept the births of children and good health as the normal way of living. Nicholas' love for Elizabeth grew far beyond just someone who would love his children. The bond that took them through the death of Mary remained throughout the births of their three children, creating a solid family of five with more anticipated in the years ahead. Such was the case when two years later another boy, George, was born. The name would be repeated many times in the history of the Verge generations. Nicholas and

Elizabeth accepted having a family of two girls and two boys as special gifts from the hand of their God. Life was at its best.

Books of mortality were kept in England at various times during the seventeenth and eighteenth centuries especially to keep records of the plague. However, the records show that there were other causes of death, especially the sea. The sea that provided a living also took it away. It was the primary provider of life to Nicholas and his family, not just fish as food on their table, but as the means of providing for his family through his fishing business. Having two boys, he looked forward to passing the business over to them as he came closer to the time when he would not be able to manage it any longer. Now in his forty-seventh year and fully aware that the common life expectancy was not far beyond his present age, he still hoped that he would see his daughters married. Fathers may not show any favourites openly, but without any prejudice they many times have one daughter who seems to be special.

Maybe it is some characteristic that stands out such as consideration, joviality, pleasantry, ambition or acceptance. Sarah had all of these and more, but she was just five years old, so young that he probably would not see her marry. Ann, maybe, but Sarah, unlikely.

Sarah and her father cherished every moment that they spent together: times when he held her hand, when he held her above his head, times when he read to her the stories and myths that abounded in the English society, and times especially when he took her for short rides in his boat along with Ann. He was very careful not to take them if there were any appearance of winds or waves. It was on such a day that Elizabeth made it clear to the girls that it was not a day for a ride in the channel, but a day to play at home. After Ann returned home from her lessons, they played as told, including two year old John who laughed with joy at almost everything that they did. Elizabeth watched over baby George but kept the sounds of the other children within hearing, ready at any time to intervene in a scuffle, settle an argument, point out a naughty word, or just laugh with them.

Silence is not detected in an instant but rather its awareness is delayed. Elizabeth, busy with the tasks of the day, became aware that all was quiet some minutes after the sounds had ceased. She ran outside and quickly observed Ann entertaining little John, but Sarah was not in sight. She raised her eyes and saw two movements, Sarah running towards the pier, and Nicholas in his boat on his way to meet her.

Many times Elizabeth had watched as Nicholas came toward the shore from another day of duty, and many times, she took Sarah by the hand to greet him. Each time it was a joyful experience as she united father and daughter and shared in their glee. The channel offered many other kinds of pleasure: the reflection of fishing sheds along the shore, the endless lap of waves, the sounds of early morning voices sharing greetings, the refreshing cooling of feet on a hot summer's day, the daily chattering of townsfolk and the lullaby of the sea during the night.

Elizabeth had experienced all of these but there was no joy in this moment. She screamed for Sarah to stop, but five year olds do not look back when they are pursued, especially when they have a goal in mind to be at the finish line first. She ran with her eyes fixed on the boat with the intent of being there when Nicholas would reach out his arms to her. Her defiance of the cries from Elizabeth increased her pace toward the end of the pier. In her attempt to turn and see if her mother was near, she miscalculated the distance to the end of the pier and plunged into the icy waters of November. Nicholas was close enough to see what happened but knew that reaching her was next to impossible even when he put the boat at full speed. The decision that Elizabeth had to make was an agonizing one. Not being a swimmer, she knew that there was no likely chance that she could help Sarah, so she was torn between the risk of leaving her children without a mother and the risk of losing Sarah. She screamed for others to see her plight but it took a while before someone saw what was happening. As soon as the first one heard the cry, the pier began to fill up with people. Nicholas was close enough to see someone jump into the water, followed by others, all hoping that it was not too late. There was hope as someone pulled her from the frigid water. They responded to her cold body in the only way that they knew which was to get her warm as quickly as possible. She was rushed to the house but time was not on her side, for even before they prepared the fire it was obvious that she had died.

Ann watched it all, assuming that her sister was just hurt and would be all right in a few minutes. However, as she observed the crying of her parents and their friends it dawned upon her that Sarah was more than just hurt, she had died and they would no longer be together. The sympathizing friends finally dwindled away to leave the parents to mourn and to face the realities of comforting one another, consoling the children, preparing for a burial, and endeavouring to put some normalcy to their lives. The Priory bell tolled her death and a couple of days later the broken hearted parents wept as the churchyard reluctantly received yet another young child.

CHAPTER TWELVE: THE ULTIMATE WEDDING

Nicholas and Elizabeth consoled each other in spite of the fact that Elizabeth often blamed herself for not being more observant and then for calling Sarah which only made her run faster. Although they sorrowed over the loss of Mary and now Sarah, they recognized that such perils were part of their society in which life and death were realities. The only means of survival was to accept what was and try to forget what was not. They put limits on times of mourning for the children that died, recognizing that intense sorrow could distract them from developing a sense of security for those that remained. They deeply gave attention to their children, especially Ann who was now eight years old, six years older than John and eight years older than George. Once again the family recovered from the shocks of the past with determination to build a lasting relationship with the children that were with them and others that might be born in the years ahead. Two other children were born into the family, a girl named Elizabeth, born four years after the birth of George and a son named Nicholas two years later. The names of Elizabeth and Nicholas would continue throughout the generations to come.

Before the happy event of Ann's marriage, Nicholas experienced sorrow twice more in the death of Jarman's wife, Mary, who died in the same year that baby Nicholas was born and her husband Jarman who died four years later. They did not die of particular maladies, but because the conditions of old age overtook them. Their children laid them to rest in the churchyard of the Priory. Thus began the final stage in the lives of Nicholas and Elizabeth.

Up to this point in the life of Nicholas, he had married his first wife, Elizabeth, some twenty years ago and his second wife, Elizabeth, sixteen years ago. Both children from his first marriage had died, one in childbirth, and the other with smallpox. His second born daughter from his second marriage had also died from drowning. After his last child was born he lived a very satisfying life for some seventeen years. He watched his children swiftly move through the stages of childhood, schooling, and teen years and in the case of Ann, marriage. Nicholas felt a tinge of guilt when he thought of how he had looked forward to Sarah's wedding more than Ann's even though she was older than Sarah, but he was also overjoyed that he could walk Ann down the aisle of the Priory. The marriage of Ann brought back memories of his second marriage to Elizabeth Christophers. It was Elizabeth's brother, John, who brought Nicholas and Elizabeth together, and now John's son would be marrying their daughter, Ann. Even though this was not an arranged marriage, both sets of parents had an informal agreement that John and Ann would be married even though the young couple were cousins.

This would be the fifth Verge wedding to take place in the Priory. There was the wedding of Jarman and Mary, the two weddings of Nicholas, the wedding of Jarman's son, John, and now Nicholas' daughter, Ann. Nicholas had been part of all of these and this time he made every effort to make it the greatest celebration of all. This anticipated marriage was the highest point in the life of the Verge family, the ultimate peak of elation, the highest expression of solidarity and the healing balm of all the wounds of the past. The siblings of Ann ranged from eight to sixteen, old enough to understand what marriage meant, especially her brother John who was sixteen and who watched all things carefully for when his time arrived. Nicholas provided help for the wedding without hesitation, making sure that John and Ann were married in the finest of style. Elizabeth weaved cloth for the most excellent of clothing to make their daughter stand out above other brides. In keeping with the tradition, the marriage was set for November, a time when crops provided plenty of food for the wedding feast. There was much to be done in preparation for the wedding. Ann chose her cousin, Charity, her best friend Evangeline and two other friends as her attendants, and John chose Ann's brother, John, his best friend George, and two other friends. Bouquets of flowers were ordered, the menu was decided upon, decorations were prepared for the Priory, transportation for the bride was reserved, the wedding dress was chosen, invitations were distributed, and a myriad of other details were taken care of.

There was a chill in the air on the wedding day, typical of a Christchurch cool morning that lasted into the afternoon, but without rain. The attendants came early to the Priory to await the arrival of the bride, as the carriage carrying her made its way through the cobblestone streets. Nicholas had told her many times about his first wife, Elizabeth, being the first bride in the town to be driven to the Priory in a carriage. Ann now experienced the same feeling of royalty herself that the first Elizabeth had decades earlier.

The grand old Priory was prepared for a happy occasion, with festoons carefully placed along the aisles, not in such a way to take the attention off the procession, but rather to blend with the colors of the bride's apparel to make her even more stunning. After the attendants took their place at the altar, and after a pause of silence, the great pipes resounded with a cheerful wedding song to welcome the entrance of the bride. Family and friends, young lads and ladies, brides in waiting, eager mothers, commoners, high society members and folks from all around filled the Nave for the wedding of the decade. They all turned to watch the bride slowly making her way to the front where she would be met by her waiting groom. John and all others that watched her procession to the altar were overwhelmed with the beauty of her train, the ribbons, lace, blending colors, and a crocheted horseshoe attached to the gown as a symbol of good luck. Her ringlets of hair flowed downward to her neck and rested upon her shoulders that were exposed by the gown that she had chosen. The musician, inspired by the magnificence of the moment, set the pipes in motion as the choir sang a lofty love song, introducing the bride and groom. The vows were simply a statement that they would commit themselves to one another as husband and wife and then came the pronouncement from the Vicar that they were married. As they proceeded from the Priory, wheat was thrown over them as a symbol of prosperity, a token that did not always work in the town of Christchurch where the wedding feast did not represent the meals upon the unseen tables. John took his new bride to the homestead of Nicholas and Elizabeth and carried her over the threshold into their new life together.

CHAPTER THIRTEEN: SHORTENED LIVES

This was the only wedding of their children that Nicholas and Elizabeth would see. However, the memory of the event was multiplied as their grandchildren and the children of John and Susannah were born.

When his young nephew, John, in his teen years came to visit he would speak of things that Nicholas found strange and that brought back the memories of his parents speaking of other Verge families in Britain. His son, George was just three years younger than John and both of them were intrigued with the things that were being said, not just about Verges in Britain, but about territories beyond their country in new found lands where fishermen went to fish in the summer. Nicholas entered the conversations at times without much enthusiasm about the thought that his children would move from the town of his birth. He tried to get promises from them that this would not happen, but he lived out his final years with some anxiety that it would.

Reaching his seventh decade took him far beyond life expectancy, making him a patriarch of his times, a mouthpiece of wisdom to his children, a bard of the town, a devout member of the Priory and a puritan voice to his society. He did not banish his thoughts of sorrow, but rather placed them in the context of the overall experience of life which made room for many thoughts of joy and celebration. With so few years left, he did not anticipate any other sorrows, but rather dwelt upon his legacy and gave time to preparing his children and grandchildren for their place in society.

However, things did not work out as he had planned, for as darkness descends quickly at noon, announcing an impending storm, so did the unhappy events descend upon the whole family. The measure of mourning depends primarily upon the relationship and age of family members. Nicholas and Elizabeth had reached the age of accepting each other's impending death. Their children also accepted the fact that when their parents became aged they should be resigned to their passing. The matter of which parent is mourned most depends upon the relationship established by each offspring. It is quite different when parents have to mourn for their children for it seems that there is no way to prepare for this. It is quite different from the way that siblings mourn for one another. They seem to be able to avoid the intensity of the mourning that parents experience for their children.

The presence of impending death came upon four members of the Nicholas Verge family in a way that touched all relationships and ages. They were just three persons, but many relations: A grandmother, a grandfather, a mother, a father, a young mother, a young wife, an older sister, a young sister, all whose lives were tightly interwoven.

It's strange how death is not ordered by age. Fairness would arrange it according to the passing of years, with the old first and the young last, but not this time. The first was just a teen, greatly cherished by all of the Verge families. Betty, the daughter of John and Susannah, came down with an illness that brought back memories of William, Joanne and Mary. John and Susannah experienced the same frustration that Nicholas and Elizabeth did in trying to get a diagnosis. Betty was sixteen years of age, with one older sibling, three younger ones, three younger cousins and many friends. She was at the center of all of the children's activities, full of energy, lovable, conscientious in her studies, and secretly chosen by many parents to be their son's wife. Her passing would place an enormous gap in her household and her town. Although Nicholas and Elizabeth were not direct grandparents of Betty, they entered into the deep sorrow that Jarman and Mary would be feeling had they not passed away some six years earlier.

The progression of Betty's illness was spasmodic, but every low was more intense than the other: long days after long nights and long nights after long days. The situation was even more difficult due to the fact that Betty's mother,

Susannah, was pregnant. Two events were imminent but there was no way to determine which would be first. Every effort was made to reverse Betty's illness, but nobody could even clearly reach a satisfactory diagnosis. Susannah's baby was born during one of Betty's highs. She seemed to have intentionally made herself strong for the event so that the family could celebrate the coming of the baby. The birth went well and on the following Sunday the family made their way to the Priory to enjoy another baptism, naming her Sarah in memory of the Sarah who had so tragically drowned. Soon after the baptism Betty succumbed to her illness. The Priory bells tolled once more and the town wept. As if knowing about this event, one hundred years later a Canadian poet would write:

Easily to the old opens the hard ground.
But when youth grows cold, and red lips have no sound,
Bitterly does the earth open to receive
And bitterly do the grasses in the churchyard grieve.

CHAPTER FOURTEEN: THE END OF AN ERA

Four years later John, the son of Nicholas noticed that his mother, Elizabeth began to express a concern about how the children would get along without their parents, which was a common topic of conversation, but in this case there was a sense of urgency in the words of his mother. John mentioned it to his other siblings and they watched for signs that there might be reason for her concern. She was a decade younger than Nicholas, but in the context of the times, she had reached old age, however with few signs to show it. All of the children and grandchildren expected Nicholas to die first in that he had lived beyond normal old age and was showing signs of decreasing strength. But now there was a concern that Elizabeth saw herself as the first to go. The strain of giving birth to seven children in a span of twenty years, the depths of sorrow of losing her step-daughter, Mary and her daughter, Sarah, the hardships of raising children in limited homemaking conditions, and fighting the many diseases that came her way, all took a toll on her. Knowing that her time was fast approaching, she diligently went about preparing the things necessary for the children and to make sure that Nicholas would not be burdened with them. She took comfort in the fact that Ann was married and that the other children were in their early adulthood and teen years.

It was as if she had planned the time of her passing. She made herself as busy as she could, knitting and sewing for the children and openly talking to Nicholas about how to prepare meals, encouraging him to avoid proud independence and to seek the care of the children. So on a cloudy Sunday morning as the Verge families made their way to the Priory, it became evident that the walk was too much for Elizabeth, and she returned to her home with her husband Nicholas at her side and accompanied by the youngest child, Nicholas. Upon arrival to their house, she sat down in her favourite chair, the chair in which she sat many times in silence after sending the children off to school and Nicholas to his work place. It was there that she had watched all of them take the same path until they diverged into their separate directions. She then thumbed through the tattered family Bible and found verses that were plain and comforting. And so it was that she was now sitting there again with all of these memories before her. Her husband, Nicholas, and her youngest son, Nicholas, led her to her bed to rest until her family returned from the Priory, but her rest upon the bed became an eternal rest as she quietly passed into another home. The bells of the Priory tolled again for yet another member of the Verge family and a few days later Elizabeth was buried in the Priory churchyard.

The family was aware that soon Nicholas would join her, not as a moment of great sorrow, but rather as an expected event that would bring the family once again to the Priory. Nicholas also accepted his fate, finding solace in the fact that he would leave a family knitted together with great care for one another and also with the assurance that they were in good health.

However, he had one request. He longed to walk once more to the place near the Priory where he had found solace so many times. The family hesitated, wondering if he could make the journey, but in the end they decided that it should be. His last child, Nicholas, now seventeen years of age knew the path well and accompanied him along the shoreline with its ceaseless lapping waves; onto the bank with its bushes, crags, and flora; up an incline that broadened his view; across a meadow where cows and horses quietly nibbled the damp morning grass; past the ruins of the old castle; across the great Priory walkways, and then to his place where the rivers Stour and Avon meet.

As spouses grow old they each accept the death of the other, but they never accept the death of a child, even if that child has grown old too. Ann was the first child of Nicholas and Elizabeth and had married John Christophers just a few years before her mother died. Along with her young children and her siblings, she knew that her father would not be with them much longer. At the beginning of her thirty-first year which was the year following her mother's funeral, she became aware that all was not well within her body. Each day she experienced dizzy spells, tiredness and acute pain but hesitated to make her illness known to her siblings, her young children or her father. Her husband, John, was the only one who knew about her condition, which placed him in the difficult situation of making the decision as to when she should consult a medical person which would sound the alarm to all. As this was taking place, her father was getting weaker as the days passed by. John was torn between waiting until Nicholas died before he would announce the condition of Ann, or announce it now and prepare Nicholas for the sad news of the impending death of his beloved daughter, the one who kept the memories of Elizabeth alive in his heart. John leaned upon the providence of God for a solution. Just days before he knew that Ann's condition should be made known, Nicholas drifted into a semiconscious state in which he remained until after his daughter died. Ann's condition rapidly declined and John made it known to all with the relief of not having to reveal it to Nicholas. She died surrounded by her husband, children, siblings, cousins, nephews and nieces. The Verge family once again assembled at the great Priory to say farewell to another beloved family member. She was laid to rest beside her mother, Elizabeth, with just a few more days to await her father.

Nicholas died as his brother Jarman had, not with pain or suffering but with the slowing of strength, weariness of mind and waning of life. One quiet evening just before sunset a stillness came over the body of Nicholas which being noticed by his children, led them to speak closely to his ear. There was no response; Nicholas had quietly left them. Just two days later he was taken on his last journey to the Priory, taking somewhat the same route that he had taken many times when he walked to his place of solitude. It was here in the grand old Priory that he had experienced the joys of the baptism of his children, the excitement of his marriages, the marriage of Ann, and the sadness of the death of his first wife and his children. "For whom the bell tolls", a phrase from the writings of Donne, had become embedded in English idioms to express the fact that all will die. The church bell tolled, simply saying that Nicholas' time had come. The pipes played and the choir sang a song composed by Isaac Watts and published just sixteen years before Nicholas died:

> Before the hills in order stood,
> Or earth received her frame,
> From everlasting Thou art God,
> To endless years the same.

It seemed as if the whole town was at the graveside that day as they laid him to rest. Somewhere in that churchyard there stands a stone weathered by age with an invisible script that reads, "Nicholas Verge born 1665, died 1735".

PART TWO:

JOHN AND HONORA

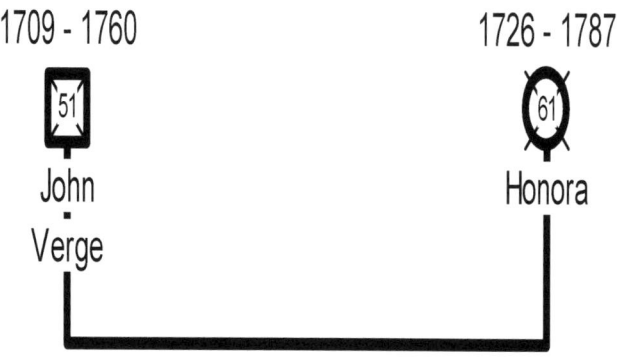

CHAPTER FIFTEEN: THE LURE OF THE OCEAN

The need of fathers to have some say in the aspirations of their sons seemed to be very present in eighteenth century England, especially when their sons were establishing their vocations. This was very evident in the life of John Junior as he was making plans for his future. Although he spent a number of years with his father in the fisheries business, and had saved enough money to attend university he had no interest in pursuing more education. Two factors made him feel that way. He became very interested in the fishing industry and looked forward to having his own business. Also, he was keenly interested in the stories about the lands across the sea and the abundance of fish there. The lure of the ocean, the thrill of the journey to a new land, a more independent life and the possibility of more affluence all pulled him away from a career in Christchurch to a vocation across the sea.

This created a tension between him and his father, especially when John Junior talked about fishing across the ocean. John recalled the conversation between John Junior and his cousins when they were younger, but he had hoped that such ideas had been forgotten. Susannah also hoped that those thoughts would have vanished from her son's mind, but there were conversations all over Christchurch about the ships that were sailing from a nearby town called Poole. It was just a few miles away and with travel increasing in the area it was easy to learn of what was happening in the whole region.

The story of Poole and its connection with the new lands began more than a century before John Junior was born. Ships in the late sixteenth century sailed there in the summer to fish and returned home during the winter. Early in the seventeenth century, communities were established, which offered a permanent way of life to those who decided to remain there. The towns were given names such as Trinity, Whitbourne and Bonaventure. Long before these were named, the island itself was called Newfoundland by its discoverer John Cabot. Towns in England, France and other countries connected with those communities in Newfoundland, creating a regular trade between Poole and the towns in Trinity Bay.

Those stories raised John Junior's interest in pursuing another world. One such story came from a fellow fisherman who had a brother that had gone to Trinity Bay for the summer and was returning to live there year around. He told of the excitement of preparing for the journey with his friends, the promises of an unusual catch, the merriment of the voyage with fiddles and songs to break the monotony of the trip, and most of all the change in his life from boredom to diversity. He described the many types of ships that traversed the ocean: Brig, Balinger, Clipper, Argosy, and Schooner. Their lengths were eighty to one hundred feet, had three or four masts and were anywhere from four hundred to eight hundred tons. Crew and passengers sometimes amounted to seventy persons.

This all increased John Junior's desire to join one of those journeys, but he could not freely express it because of the opposition from his parents. He also wondered how he could set up a new life in a new land without a wife. He was in his mid-twenties, the average age for marriage, but to this point he was uncertain of whether he should go to this new land and marry someone there or marry at home and take his new wife with him. He learned that there were a few single women in that place known as Trinity Bay. Up to this time men went there to fish for the summer, and returned home for the winter. However, communities were developing, and families were being established. If he were to wait until a suitable wife arrived he might become older than his plan for marriage.

Far from Christchurch there was a little community in Ireland called Phillipstown, one of many plantation towns of mid seventeenth century Ireland. Among the workers on the plantation was a young woman of sixteen years, trying to eke out an existence within the economic plight of the nation. Her name, Honora, a very common Irish name, meant honor, a word that she tried to live up to. Her life appeared hopeless as she routinely worked long hours, receiving just enough to take care of herself and her family. However, she had spirit and promised herself that she would never allow adversity to control her life. She would seek some unconventional way of turning her life around, although at the moment she did not know what it was. Walking to her home one evening, she glanced at a poster on the wall of the town hall with the word NEWFOUNDLAND accented. She kept walking, but recalling that she had heard about this place before, she quickly turned back to see what the message was about. It was simply an invitation for young women to become house servants in the new communities that were being established across the ocean. Honora's first response was to dismiss the thought, but then she became curious and took a second look. Journeys afar always sparked interest in the youth of Phillipstown, especially when they assessed their future. The lure of crossing the ocean to a new world fascinated them and dropped a measure of hope in their lives. Honora spent the remainder of her walk trying to determine how such a journey would change her life.

Back in his home in Christchurch, John Junior was dwelling upon how his journey to a new world would ever come about. He wanted to make the decision soon but he was always confronted with the matter of marriage. His latest decision was to find out more information on the fishery trade with Newfoundland and connect with his friend's brother to see exactly how he felt about it. His new friend saw it as an overwhelmingly positive experience, especially the financial return. He spoke of the waters that teemed with fish, the vastness of Trinity Bay and the inlets that were designed for communities. He told John Junior about the young single women that sometimes arrived there to serve in the households that were being established. His friend shared his plans to return to Trinity Bay, get married and remain there. John Junior became more motivated than ever to pursue his goal of becoming a habitant of one of the Trinity Bay communities. He knew that it would be difficult to tell his parents, but he had his mind made up.

His father sternly made it clear that he was a disappointment to the whole family and that his plans were not rational. His mother wept because he was going and also wept because he was going without the blessing of the family. John Junior began to check out the crossings and made preparations to seek passage in one of the next ships that would leave from Poole. Seeing that he was determined to make the journey, his parents reluctantly accepted his decision. His friend coached him on how to behave in the company of sailors, the ship's crew and the ladies that were on board. He was also forthright in describing the challenges of crossing the ocean and adapting to the rugged way of living.

Back in the little Irish town of Phillipstown, Honora was fluctuating between answering the advertisement that was on her mind ever since she first saw it. The right time to discuss her plans with her parents came in the least expected way at the end of a work day that lasted late into the night. Some would call it coincidental, others fate, and a few, God's sovereignty. Her parents saw her tiredness as she reached the house and commented on the unfairness of the work demands of the plantation. They expressed hope that someday she would find a better life. Honora took advantage of the moment to tell them all about the posted message and how she was reacting to it. There was silence when she finished as both parents glanced at each other to see who would be first to respond in a positive way. Both nodded and her father asked how she felt. Honora was quick to tell them that she was ready to pursue this new way of life, even with all of the stories of things that went very wrong. The parents held her hand and simply nodded their understanding. Honora never looked back. Not long after, she visited the recruiting office and signed up for the first ship that would leave Cork in the spring. There was nothing else left to do but wait.

John Junior's waiting was over. His name was placed on the log for the departure of The Rainbow, a ship due to sail to Trinity Bay, Newfoundland. Having been called John Junior to prevent confusion within the family, he was glad to register himself as John, a name that he would use from now on. He had just two weeks to get ready for the journey. He would need blankets, clothing for the chilly winds, a secure trunk, a survival kit, and secret weapons in case of pirates. He also would take a Bible given to him by his mother.

The most difficult part of all was saying goodbye to his parents and siblings. Nobody mentioned the greatest concern of all, but it was there in the silence. After tears, prayers, and fears, the final words of good-bye were spoken and John turned to go. As he walked to his carriage, his brother, Joseph, quietly whispered to him that he also was thinking about taking a voyage to the new land but didn't know how to approach his parents with his plans.

CHAPTER SIXTEEN: JOHN AND HONORA MEET

The departure day in Poole had just a bite of March in it as the crew and passengers made their way to The Rainbow, a ship that had plied those waters many times. The saying was that Captain Durell could tell from the passengers the kind of journey that it would be. He observed the passengers' state of health, listened to their demands, glanced at the way they were dressed, and watched how they conversed with one another. His judgment was that if the weather cooperated, this would be a pleasant sail.

John found his way to his berth, which because of his age and obvious strength, happened to be on the upper deck. He was the sort of fellow that could be called upon in a crisis, and who would gladly work to help reduce his fare. He had studied the route from charts that he borrowed from some sailor friends, so he looked forward to seeing the journey unfold. He detected a slow movement of the ship away from the pier and realized that he was on his way to the great unknown.

The beginning of Honora's trip was quite different from that of John's. The coach from Phillipstown to Cork was a long and arduous journey, not just because of the distance which sometimes took up to a week, but because of the diversity of passengers. Some were criminals that were being sent to places across the sea as a punishment for their crimes. When necessary, they were made to push the coach through difficult terrain and were always made to walk up the hills. They did all of this chained to one another and to the carriage. The coach was open sided and the passengers sat on the sides with their backs to one another, limiting conversation to the person seated next to them. Honora was between a sailor and a priest, both going on the same ship that she was. The sailor, who had travelled much, kept the conversation away from such things as food, weather, and pirates and tried to dwell upon "good times" using language that would be more direct, had not the presence of the priest silently moderated it. When they reached the ship, she quickly lost herself from the sailor and tried to keep the priest in sight.

Single young men and women were called "youngsters", a label that placed them between those who were looked upon as irresponsible and those who would be made responsible. Not many youngsters could pay the full fare, so they were given tasks to make up for it, not just little tasks but those that were below the dignity of the crew. The way that they were treated motivated them to make friends with one another, not just for friendship but for their security. Honora kept all of this in her mind as she remembered the conversation of the sailor on the coach.

Her ship sailed from Poole enroute to Trinity Bay, Newfoundland and stopped at Cork to pick up youngsters and criminals. It spent just one day there and passengers from Poole were not permitted to leave the ship. There was a hive of activity as new passengers were registered and sent to their berths. Of the sixty persons on board, the younger men from Poole and the youngsters from Cork represented one third of these on the ship. All was in place as the sun was setting on the harbor of Cork casting slanting shadows over the tall ships as they prepared for their departure. Honora watched as each one silently slipped from its pier in the same way that The Rainbow had nudged itself into the channel.

Sailing ships were victims of the winds. Older ships could only sail in the direction of the wind, but the newer ones with added masts and more sails could sail into the wind. However, they were slowed significantly when this occurred. Needless to say there were very few times when the conditions were perfect. At the start The Rainbow had the wind in her favor, leaving Cork behind until it became a speck on the horizon.

Three hours out from the harbour Honora experienced the dreaded seasickness that her friends had told her about. She prayed that it would be just a passing ailment but it remained with her, sometimes severe and sometimes manageable. Youngsters were not pitied nor coddled; they were simply told to live with it. Honora had studied the voyage, so she knew that it could possibly be three to four weeks, but with delays and storms it could take up to five or six, either of which was long when seasickness prevailed.

At nightfall passengers began to find their way to the appointed places for sleeping. The accommodations were dormitory style: a large number of beds in one area for males, another for females, and private rooms for married couples. The crew had their own section of the ship and the prisoners were kept in chains in a room situated deeper below deck.

It was a quiet night and even Honora felt much better the next morning. She waited for breakfast with some sense of apprehension. She had heard about the pork that was salted and packed into barrels, salted and dried fish, bags of oats and cornmeal for porridge, and, of course, the ship's biscuit, bread dried so hard that it was almost impossible to chew. Breakfast was simply a bowl of porridge and very weak tea. Meals would be the greatest challenge of her voyage.

John made known to the crew his history of fishing with his father and his knowledge of sailing. In exchange for a reduction in his fare, he was given tasks such as helping with the sails, sweeping the deck, keeping watch for other ships and predicting storms. His berth was set up so that he could take part in any emergencies that might arise. He was not aware of the Irish youngsters until he was well into the journey. Even though he saw more of them than he expected, he did not inquire as to why they were on the ship. However, one day out of curiosity, he asked one of the young ladies what they would be doing in Trinity Bay. Her answer was quite long as if it were therapeutic to tell of the condition of the towns that they came from and why so many responded to the need for young women to be servants in the new land.

Traversing the Atlantic in a sailing ship in the eighteenth century exposed passengers to treatment that was beyond cruel. The law of the ship was heartless as was the conscience of those who meted out the punishments. Walking the plank to their eternal destination was the plight of any that broke the law. Passengers, who had never been exposed to such injustice, tried to turn away from the sight but were made to look upon the event so that they would be cautious in their deeds. In many ships, stealing the least little morsel, harming a person, fostering mutiny, disobeying the ship's rules, or dishonoring the captain could mean death. Minor refractions could result in being placed in irons for the rest of the journey, deprived of food to a starving level, and heavy labor or very high fines.

It was dangerous to tell on another person, especially if the culprit were a crew member. Honora came close to being caught up in such a situation one day when she saw a young man trying to adjust one of the smaller sails to the wind. It got torn in the process which probably would not have been noticed had not a sailor passed by at that very moment. He was not one of kind disposition and to make things worse, he was a little inebriated. He violently kicked the young man and then hit him furiously, sending him against the rail. Knowing that someone could have seen him, the sailor departed the area in haste. Having compassion upon the young man, Honora ran towards him to offer what help she could, but he desperately waved her away, motioning that the sailor might return. She turned back in tears, trying to understand what kind of justice system really existed or if one existed at all.

Honora was disturbed all through the night by the sight of the young man in pain, even to the point of sobbing at times. It occurred to her that he was the same man who had asked her what she would be doing in Trinity Bay. She set her mind to find him and carefully looked for a safe time to strike up a conversation but without any reference to his event with the sailor.

As passengers made their way to their berths, it was common to have short conversations, maybe a reference to their day, their thoughts of home, the weariness of the seas and many other topics. Honora glanced at a young man on his way to his deck berth and noticed that he glanced at her. She recognized him as the man who had asked her about her work and also the person who had been hit by the sailor. During their short conversation John quietly conveyed thanks for her concern regarding his episode with the sailor. In an amazing turn of events, John Verge met the Irish girl, Honora. Destiny had even more in store for them.

CHAPTER SEVENTEEN: THE STORM

The route from Cork to Trinity Bay was approximately 1800 miles and fairly direct. Food was meted out carefully and if there were any signs of an impending storm it was rationed. There was not much boredom because everybody toiled so much they were happy to rest for the night. However, there was some entertainment, especially singing Irish songs and dancing after the evening meal. The dancing could be crude at times if the sailors had sipped too much ale, but they were overlooked if they did not start any trouble. The young danced too, but with a measure of uneasiness less they spend too much time away from their chores. John and Honora developed a happy relationship, carefully making sure that they did not take advantage of the opportunities afforded them. They shared information regarding their backgrounds, his difficulty of getting permission from his parents, and her ease of receiving support from hers. They both agreed that the loneliest part of the journey was not being able to contact their parents. However, their times together began to fill that gap even to the point that the need for their parents was being replaced by their need for one another. Even though there were some years between them, their feelings for each other grew deeper as they spent more time together.

The ideal voyage of a sailing ship seldom exists, which is true for this journey of The Rainbow. Honora was in a deep sleep when the clanging suddenly awakened her. From the beginning of the voyage, passengers were warned that they should stay in their berths until they were informed of what was happening. In this case the tossing of the ship was evidence that a storm had quickly come up, which made the passengers quite anxious to see what was going on. Honora's first concern was not about herself, but of John who would be among the first to take his position on deck. John did just that with great concern as to whether the ship's sails could be eased enough to lower the pressure of the wind upon the ship. The sailors were quick to loosen the lines to keep The Rainbow from leaning to the point of no return. All of this had to be done while the vessel was being tossed to and fro in mountainous seas. Below deck passengers prepared to respond to whatever command came from the captain even if it meant staying in accommodations that were quickly becoming less than sanitary because of the acute seasickness.

Mariners of long ago had many ways to predict a coming storm. Ship's logs were kept of each voyage to record patterns of the clouds, winds, rain, ice, and snow. Also, seasoned sailors leaned upon their memories to forecast what weather was coming next. There was nothing of absolute certainty though, for nature is always filled with surprises. Thus was the plight of The Rainbow. Evening had fallen with a sense of stillness, as if the night assured them that all was well, but it was not so. The watchman from the crow's nest observed that the stars had suddenly disappeared, as if a dark blanket appeared between the ship and the sky. Thunder rumbled, lightening flashed and torrents of rain fell from the darkened clouds. The vessel was without warning as if this act of nature attacked it with intent. The watchman's urgent cry brought sailors running to their posts, seemingly becoming awake as they ran. John was at his post in seconds, at first reliving the event of the torn sail, but he quickly banished that from his mind so that he would have full confidence for the task ahead. He felt strength from Honora and knew that she was awake and praying fervently that he would be protected from harm.

The storm did not come for just a fleeting moment neither did it spare the crew. The seamen, as if at war, tried with all their might to furl the sails before the winds would turn the vessel upside down. John, being thrown to and fro, felt the tearing of his flesh as he wrapped the lines around his hand. After the sails were furled and everything was secured, there was not much that the crew could do but watch the feud between The Rainbow and the waves. Not everybody escaped the mountains of water that washed over the ship. Captain Durell had given strict orders that no passengers should go on deck, but orders did not assuage the fear of some. In their state of panic they made their way to the deck as if to find more refuge there, but only to be met with the force of violent waves that washed them quickly into the sea. Honora, in her distress of seasickness, fear and concern for John was tempted to see what was happening above. She vacillated between riding out the storm and trying to see John. After many hours of incessant pounding of doors, unspeakable sickness and unimaginable creaking, she decided to go, but only for a moment, for she suddenly realized the consequences of defying a command of the captain. Realistically, all that she could do was to pray and wait.

It seems that if a storm comes quickly it leaves quickly, depending upon the speed of travel. After two long days the storm began to abate at a pace that brought the ship back in shape. It was late afternoon of the second day that permission was given for passengers and sailors alike to return to the deck and line up for the evening meal of salted beef and ship's biscuits. Honora swiftly made her way to meet with John for their daily conversation. She scanned the deck, looked into the riggings to see if he were still setting the sails, searched through the line-up in case he might be looking for her, and inquired of others about him. With a heavy heart and great discouragement she began to make her way back to her berth to process all of the emotions that enveloped her. These emotions were about to be reversed, for John, after searching the deck, made his way to the ladder and just before he arrived he saw her placing her foot upon the first step. He called her name in the same endearing way that he would say it for years to come, and she responded accordingly.

The storm had passed. Sails were returned to full mast, the litter was cleared from the deck, berths were restored to order and the mess hall put back together. There was much lightheartedness as the ship's compass was adjusted to set its course for Trinity Bay, with expectations that the arrival would be less than a week away.

At sunrise the morning after the storm, the captain called together all of those onboard, including the criminals, to pay respect to those who were lost on those two fateful nights.

John and Honora spent as much time together as possible during those last few days. Neither of them knew exactly where they would be living when they reached the end of their journey. John's intention was to remain with the fishermen during the summer and become a planter when the ship returned to Poole. Honora was to meet a family and become a servant for them.

At dawn on a clear spring's morning a booming voice from the crow's nest announced that land was in sight, bringing everybody to the deck apart from the forgotten criminals in the hole. As the ship came closer, the passengers began to make an assessment of this land that they had never seen before, isolated with few houses and blanketed with snow. This settlement of Trinity had a population of some sixty persons, made up of fishermen who decided to stay throughout the winters with their families and become settlers. Their rough wooden framed houses appeared one by one as The Rainbow neared the landing place.

Being one of the fishing crew, John would live on the ship until just before it returned to Poole in the fall, which was of great convenience to him, but not to Honora. She would only be able to see him at times when he returned from the fishing grounds. She was chosen by a couple at the dock to be their servant to manage the house and care for the children while the parents worked in the fisheries trade.

Honora would have found life in Trinity Bay unbearable had it not been that John would be seeing her from time to time throughout the summer. The challenges of living in such harsh conditions and taking care of four children made her wonder at times if she had made the right decision in leaving her family and home. However, it became routine day after day, month after month into the second year. After the ship left for Poole John found accommodations and spent the winter partly finishing a very modest home for their upcoming marriage in the first Anglican Church in Trinity. A new homestead was added to the community, one in which seven children would be born over the next two decades. John, the grandson of Jarman, had brought the Verge name to Newfoundland as others would in future generations.

CHAPTER EIGHTEEN: A GREAT TRAGEDY

There is a very sad epilogue to the story of John and Honora. Each child brought happiness to them and as was the custom, their children were given the names of parents. The first daughter was named Honora, not just as a tribute to her mother, but to keep alive the Irish legacy in the family. John's parents, John and Susannah, were ecstatic at the news and although they had not seen their daughter in law, they looked forward to someday seeing both of the Honora's. The next message to John and Susannah was the announcement of another baby on the way, hopefully a boy that would carry the name John to the third generation. After some weeks, John and Honora began to anticipate the excitement of their parents' reply. Honora projected her feelings of motherhood to her mother in law, knowing that grandmothers develop a bond with little granddaughters that can't be explained. Although grandfathers may not have the same intensity with grandsons, they do cherish every moment when the generations meet. John and Honora waited to hear of the exuberance of their parents at the news that a grandson might be on the way.

There was an unusual wait for someone to come to the door when the letter was delivered to the grandparents' home. After some minutes, a very frail lady with the appearance of premature age and a body wrecked with maladies slowly reached out her hand and nodded thanks. On the way back to the room she gently opened the letter with reticence, knowing that bad news would make matters worse in the midst of their calamities and good news would only last for a season. The message was as she was expecting; another child was to be added to their many grandchildren. She agonized over whether her husband would benefit from the news, or die with the pain of knowing that he would never see the child. Smallpox does not negotiate with circumstances. The appointed time to finish its battle with the husband and wife would arrive as part of the course. She slowly made her way to him, hoping that wisdom would direct her to do the right thing, but nature left her with no need of making such a decision. His broken and spotted body was beyond listening to messages, for he had entered that stage where distress and pain were fading away. Although Susannah knew that his body should not be touched, she also knew that it didn't matter anymore. She knelt before him, gently held his head in her arms, and read the message to him.

"Our dearest mother and father, we read with joy your response to our announcement of the birth of Honora. Her presence blessed our home and we knew that you were also sharing in that blessing. She has been well and growing day by day. She is even into mischief, the kind that you would find humorous rather than worrisome. We look forward to that time when it becomes possible for all of us to be together. We know father that you relish the relationship that you and your son developed and how such a relationship would repeat itself with the hopeful coming of a grandson. It is with great delight that we announce that another child is on

the way. We are praying deeply that a son will be born to us and we will assure you that he will be named John, carrying the name to the third generation. We know that there are many irregularities in the mailing system, so let us know as soon as you receive this. By that time our child will be born. We trust that all is well and that you are in good health."

After her husband's body was collected she sat and wrote:

"My dearest children, it is with great sadness that I send you this message. My heart aches that I should bring such sorrow to you, especially near the occasion of another birth. Your dear father has been suffering greatly in the last few weeks as he fought a battle against the dreaded smallpox. My heart weeps to tell you that your message reached us just as he was passing from this life to another. I read your letter to him, knowing that he did not receive your news, which may have been the better for him. How dreadful would it have been for him to hear about the child, knowing that he would

never share joyful moments with him. But I am sure that you will pass on to the little one how his grandfather loved all of you so much. My dears I have but more sadness to tell you, with hope that you will be strong enough to bear these tidings. I have been in the same battle with your dear father and my time is very short. By the time that you receive this message I will be with him in that land that lets no sorrow in. I send you a hug my dear Honora and John, and a special hug and kiss to my dearest grand-daughter. May God heal the sorrows of your hearts and fill your home with joy."

A few days later Susannah died and was laid to rest beside her husband in the Priory Churchyard. Their grandson, John, was born just a few days after the death of his grandparents. Many other children were born to John and Honora during the mid-years of the eighteenth century, establishing the first Verge clan on the island of Newfoundland.

John's younger brother, Joseph, felt the call of the sea and he kept his last words to John that he would be next to cross the ocean. Unlike John,

Joseph married a lady in Christchurch, Sarah Keay and brought her and one or two of his children with him. After John died Joseph became a father figure to John's and Honora's children and enjoyed a loving, caring relationship with all of them. Other children were born in Trinity Bay. They settled in Nova Scotia and Boston and raised families there bringing the Verge clan all the way from Christchurch, England to lands that their forefathers did not know existed.

PART THREE:

GEORGE AND JOSEPH

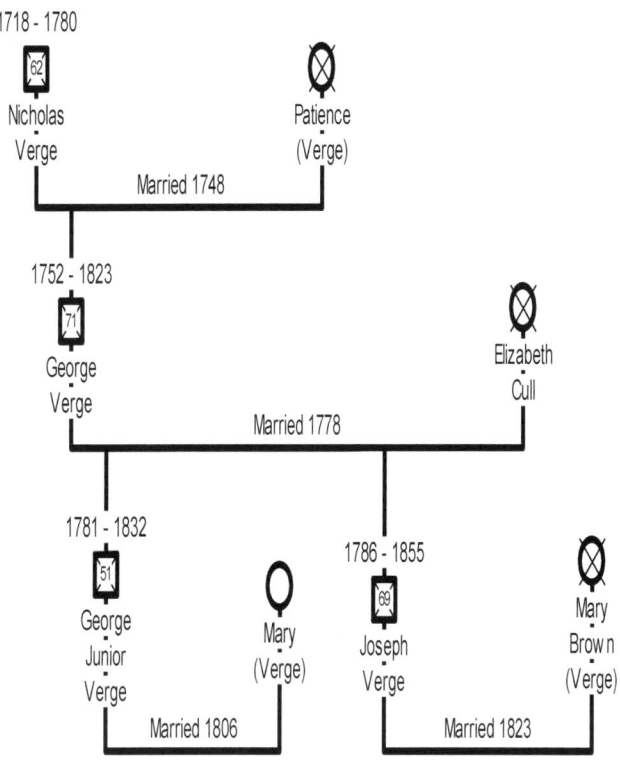

CHAPTER NINETEEN: A CHILD AT CHRISTMASTIME

The Christmas of 1769 was memorable for Nicholas, the son of Nicholas and Elizabeth. He and his wife, Patience, discovered that their son, George and his fiancée, Elizabeth, were expecting a child immediately after the twelve days of Christmas. This was of concern to the parents. George, just seventeen years of age, was not able to provide a home for his future bride and their expected baby. George was the second youngest of the family, but the first to establish a serious relationship with a woman. They had no intention of being married until George was nineteen or twenty and able to provide for a wife and children. However, things did not go that way when they discovered that Elizabeth was pregnant. Nicholas and Patience were crushed at the thought that George would be married at such a young age, so they pressured him to wait until after the baby was born, making him at least eighteen. In their eyes he was not prepared to be a father and certainly felt that the economic situation was impossible. However, a number of factors in the society added to this scenario. If the parents married before the child was born he became legitimate. However, if the marriage took place after the birth, the child was tagged illegitimate. This scenario was not an option for the parents so they reversed the thought of delaying the marriage and prepared for a wedding right after the Christmas celebrations.

Regardless of the situation, Christmas was celebrated with all of the family traditions. Knowing that Elizabeth would become George's wife, Nicholas and Patience welcomed her to the Christmas celebrations and treated her as one of the family. She helped with the early preparation of food for the twelve days of feasting, among which were Christmas cakes, minced pies, cookies, sweet breads and various cheeses. It was decided that a goose would be the center of the Christmas platter. Their home was decorated with tinsel, wax figures, paper mache, beads, flowers and wire ornaments. Stockings full of gifts were hung throughout the season.

Night after night at the Verge household there were games, carolling, dancing and mummering. Long chats included yarns about close to death experiences, fictitious tales of long ago, illustrious descriptions of ghosts, trolls and fairies, side-splitting jokes, and of course, the regular bits and pieces of boasting. The door was always open to friends. Each night was mirthful, not only in the Verge household, but throughout the town of Christchurch as the flow of ale increased. As the revelers marched to their homes, they experienced a mild sense of shame as they passed the great Priory with its reverential staunch and pious presence.

Nicholas and Patience were the hosts of the Christmas dinner along with Elizabeth's parents who came by invitation. The goose was seasoned with sea salt and pepper the evening before and placed in a cool place that nature provided on a late December day. Whilst the oven was being heated, the goose was stuffed with rosemary, clementine, and cinnamon sticks, and the finishing touch was to pierce the lump above the goose's breast to let the fat melt out. Potatoes were roasted, vegetables boiled, puddings steamed, sage leaves fried, sauces prepared, and ale poured.

Nicholas had used his talent of woodwork to craft a table, a work of art with carvings on each sturdy leg, invisible joints in the table top, long lasting polish, matched carvings in each chair back and very comfortable seats. The bonded families took their places at the table and sang a Christmas carol, followed by a short prayer of thanks and a hearty Merry Christmas. They dined throughout the afternoon with lots of conversation and merriment. After the meal, the breast bone of the goose was given to the two fathers to see who would get the longer piece. Nicholas prevailed and as he held the piece he wished that the coming child would be a healthy grandson for him and a son for George. His wish came true when the child was born and was given the name George, the namesake of his father.

Although it was common for elaborate public weddings to take place when the bride was pregnant, in this case the couple and their parents felt that a private ceremony would be more appropriate in light of the financial situation and the closeness to the birth which took place just after the couple were married. George Junior was born just after the New Year dawned.

As George Junior began to enter his childhood stages of crawling, walking and talking, the grandparents caught the joy of each occasion. For ten years there was only George Junior in the family of George and Elizabeth. He was the center of everybody's attention: aunts, uncles, cousins and grandparents. Nicholas spent time with him telling stories to keep him connected to the generations before him. When he came of age, he entered school and took great interest in learning. His parents did everything possible to assure him a good upbringing.

It was at this time that a dreaded enemy returned again to England, reaching its tentacles into every town in the country. Smallpox had invaded the land a number of times before and after each visit there was some hope that maybe it had been defeated. However it was as strong as ever, entering homes that had never been visited, and taking family members at random with no way to save them. The grandfather and grandson were bonded beyond any normal relationship, but the monster smallpox took both of them just three months apart. Nicholas knew that he was attacked by the dreaded disease so he hastily put his house in order, clearly writing in his will the things that his wife, sons and daughters, would receive, and especially what would be left to his only grandson, ten year old George Junior. There were provisions for his education, money towards a house for his family, a place in the wood-working business, plus unique books, carvings and his cherished watch. As he neared his end, he thought back to how he took his father, Nicholas, the patriarch of the clan, to a spot that had become sacred to the family.

However he was too weak to walk there and as he faded away the tradition of the walk faded with him. He died September 18, 1780; unbelievably and without warning his treasured ten year old grandson, George Junior died on December 12, 1780. In attempts to ward off any transmission of the disease, there were no public funerals but just the transportation of their bodies to the churchyard. The Priory bell tolled for the young and the old, as it had done decades earlier.

CHAPTER TWENTY: THE SECOND GEORGE

George and Elizabeth were still young and after a time of mourning, they decided that their home needed little feet traversing the floor again and a little tongue that would never stop talking. Just one year later nature repeated itself by giving them another son, whom they unhesitatingly named George after the George who had died. Once again there was a George Junior in the family. Four other sons were born during the next fifteen years, among whom was Joseph, five years younger than George Junior, and who would be very much part of the next event in the family.

Both George Junior and Joseph were baptised in the Priory as were their parents, grandparents and great grandparents. They were told stories of how their great grandfather, Nicholas, who as a boy, regularly walked to a spot near the Priory where he would reflect upon his life, and how before he died he asked his son, Nicholas, their grandfather, to take him to that spot for one last time. They were told the stories of the births, marriages, and deaths of aunts, uncles, nieces, nephews, and cousins, all of whom chose to live in Christchurch. Schooling was much improved since their great grandfather's day and there was more diversity of occupations. Some of the siblings turned away from the fishery and took up woodworking. However, George Junior became attached to the ocean, especially at those times when the sun reflected the surrounding hills and also because of the practical aspect of gleaning a living from its denizens. He was also enamored by the sea as a highway to exotic places around the world. He listened carefully to the stories about his second cousin, John, going to Trinity Bay some fifty years earlier, stories that fed his curiosity and inspired him to seek this new way of life. There were towns beyond Trinity Bay, many of which were becoming well established with names such as Twillingate, Harbour Grace, Placentia and, of course, the largest of all, St. John's. Other towns were similarly named by early discoverers, all of which was exciting to George Junior as he longed to explore these communities first hand, especially

Twillingate which was not permanently inhabited until the early seventeenth century when English fishermen began to settle there. Before that the French named the island Toulinquet because of its likeness to islands off France. The French presence waned at the beginning of the eighteenth century, opening up opportunities for the English to move in and set up the first community, growing from twelve families in the earlier part the century, to a booming town at the end of the century.

This information reached the town of Christchurch, sparking conversations about the sailing ships that were crossing the Atlantic Ocean to towns in Newfoundland, especially Twillingate. George Junior listened to every word and talked about it to his parents to see how they would feel about his leaving home for places across the ocean. They knew about the time when Jarman's grandsons went to Trinity Bay and how much grief their parents experienced during that time. However, messages from them and their children over the years brought comfort to the family knowing that that their children did well in the new country.

As the nineteenth century was approaching, George Junior finished school and found himself at a crossroad; he had to pursue a vocation at home or follow his dreams of crossing the ocean to lands beyond the sea. It became clear that his choice was to join a ship that was going to Twillingate. His parents became distressed at his decision, and if that were not enough, Joseph was also determined to go with George Junior even though he was five years younger than his brother. However, he was robust, hardworking and very responsible. After many agonizing discussions with their parents, the two young men were released to find a new habitation across the ocean, albeit with much hesitation. Even though they finalized their intent to go, there were many details to work through before they actually left. This raised the spirit of the parents for a year or two as their sons worked out the process of beginning their voyage.

First of all there was the matter of having finances to pay fares and accommodations while they looked for employment. Following in the steps of their grandfather, they took up woodworking. With diligent work and careful spending, they slowly saved enough money to pay for the expenses of their venture, which came at a time when the number of ships sailing to Twillingate was increasing. The town was growing fast, enticing newcomers to stay, which was the intent of George Junior and Joseph.

CHAPTER TWENTY ONE: A DIFFICULT DEPARTURE

Before George Junior could continue with his planning, there was something that he had to resolve in relation to his parents and siblings. For the first two years of his life, he was the only living child and knew nothing about his brother who had died before he was born. As he entered into his third year he overheard his parents talking about the first George who had the same name that he had. They did not tell George Junior directly, but he also heard conversations about this older George when his uncles and aunts came to visit. This was all very confusing, and he wondered if some secret was being kept from him. It came more to light when George Junior began to play with other children in the nearby homes, among which were those a little older who remembered the first George. The parents were secretive in those things, assuming that everything was better that way.

George Junior had a cousin, John, who was twelve years old when the George Junior was born. As they talked about venturing out across the ocean to other lands, he would ask John what he remembered about the other George that was born before him. John reluctantly told him as much as he could, but refrained from some information that he knew would cause George Junior to be distressed. George Junior decided to ask his mother. He would never forget the answer that he received. His mother told him all about how his older brother was born just after Christmas, ten years before George Junior was born, how much she and his father loved him, how he grew to be very intelligent, how interested he was with schooling, how he planned to be a woodworker with his father and how proud they were of him. She expressed how much they missed him, how much they mourned when he died, how much they still thought of him, and that they named their next child George to keep memories of him alive.

The information left George Junior with a multitude of questions. Was he just a replacement for his brother? Did they expect everything from him that they did from his older brother? Did they feel that his brother would never leave them as he was planning to? Were his other brothers feeling the same way? Ever since his mother told him these things, he wrestled with a myriad of feelings, including persistent guilt about going across the ocean. He was now nearing his twentieth year, the first year of the nineteenth century, both of which were landmarks for him. In himself he felt that he had reached a high level of independence and the new century ushered in an era that was changing the face of society all over the world. Steamboats were replacing sailing ships, the industrial revolution was expanding especially since the invention of the spinning jenny which was just a decade before the birth of George Junior, and travel had increased to a point where it was not a novelty anymore, taking away the concept of separation for life. He hoped that his parents and family would recognize these changes but it seemed as if they did not want to depart from the status quo. The fact that Joseph was making plans to accompany George Junior on his journey was evidence that he was an exception.

They gathered much information from those who had returned to England from Twillingate. They learned that during their young years, fish merchants had settled there which opened up opportunities for settlers to sell their catches. Their plan was to join a fishing crew until they could purchase a boat of their own. Of course, during that time they would become planters, build homes and begin families.

They had heard much about the Slade Company ships that sailed from Poole to Twillingate during the fishery trade, and also discovered that these ships were prominent in carrying settlers there. By the end of the eighteenth century there were one hundred forty men and women and one hundred and eighty children in the town. There was no church building, no schoolhouse and no minister. The adults were concerned that there was no minister to teach the gospel to the children so they wrote a letter to the Church of England to see if someone could be sent there for that purpose. George Junior and Joseph could not fathom the thought of a town without a church, after being baptized and confirmed in one of the greatest churches in England. There was no Newfoundland currency so English pounds were used in the fishing trade, but barter was also commonly used. The winters were much more severe than those in Christchurch, and vessels were lost each year. Rather than relent from going, they carefully used the information to prepare for their life in a new world. John Slade had died before 1800, but his ships were still plying the route from Poole to Twillingate well into the nineteenth century. George Junior and Joseph, who lived not far from Poole, made acquaintance with the sailors on these ships, opening a door for their departure.

It was a forlorn moment when George and Elizabeth, along with their three other children had their final discussions with George Junior and Joseph about their plans. The two boys gave the family the information that they had received from friends who had been there and others who were going. They tried to console the dread of their parents about having their sons lost at sea. Their sons refuted with the reality that a storm could do the same at home. In the midst of her emotions and without thinking, their mother cried aloud that her first son, George, would not do this to her. Realizing what she had said, she threw her arm around George Junior. He understood her feelings in that moment and as she apologized with tears, she was released from the resistance of letting him go. His father, and even the other children, accepted what had taken place and with a new understanding, they wished the brothers well with their words and prayers.

CHAPTER TWENTY TWO: DEEP THOUGHTS

The time had come to finalize the details of their departure. First they had to make a contact with one of the merchant ships that was sailing to Twillingate, which was not difficult in light of all of the ships that were busily plying their trade at that time. After John Slade and his son died, his nephew became the chief agent for the company and was very successful in placing planters in a strategic location in northern Newfoundland. George Junior and Joseph had an interest in being planters right from their decision to cross the ocean. They decided to go to Poole and remain there until they were accepted as planters, and booked on the next ship going to the Twillingate/Fogo area. In the very early beginning of the eighteenth century, on a clear March morning, one of the Slade ships began once more to sail with the rising sun behind them. On board were two brothers bringing the first generation of Verges to Twillingate, one of the oldest towns in Newfoundland.

Their ship was a brig, a common type of vessel used to transport goods from Newfoundland to England such as seal skins, beaver skins, cod fish, cod oil, salmon, oars, hoops and various kinds of wood. She was also used to carry planters to Newfoundland to procure the goods that kept the brigs in service. George Junior and Joseph, being determined to become planters, found favour among the owners and received their voyage for a nominal fee. The Delight was some one hundred feet in length and of two hundred and fifty tons. She was a two mast vessel with the ability to sail at a speed of ten knots. She sailed the Atlantic route many times during the decades just before and after the beginning of the nineteenth century, proving her endurance and long life. The brigs had many names such as Fame, Love and Unity, Stag and Delight. The brothers took it as a confirmation of their plans when they discovered they were sailing on the Delight. The persons on board were made up of the crew, those involved in the trades, a school teacher, and the planters to be, including George and Joseph. The safety of the voyages had improved significantly since their cousin John, went to Trinity Bay over sixty years ago. A new system for the fairness of the food had developed over the years of sailing. Each person on board except the captain and crew were personally given portions of food to last them throughout the voyage. They had to plan ahead in case there would be storms that would make the voyage longer and had to make sure that the food was kept in such a way that it did not spoil. George Junior and Joseph laid out plans for the protection of the food, especially to keep it from theft.

As the brig sailed out of Poole harbour the two brothers watched until their home was no longer in sight. It was a star filled night as they stood there facing the possibility of never seeing their family again. Each knew what the other was thinking but they left it unspoken. They soon pushed these thoughts aside and replaced them with the busyness of settling in for the voyage. Their berth was filled with men from Poole and its environs, all with the same anticipation but not without uncertainty. George Junior felt responsible to keep Joseph from feeling inferior because of his age. Although most of the men would encourage Joseph in times of difficulty, some would treat him as a child, especially if he showed any signs of weakness. Also, their language might intimidate a fifteen year old.

The fishing company representative that sailed with George Junior and Joseph met with them to discuss the details of becoming a planter and gave assurance that every attempt would be made to provide the necessities to get started. There were specific steps to becoming a planter, the first of which was to work as a family servant or join a fishing crew, the second of which was most common for men. Because of very low wages it sometimes took years to become a planter. The second step was marriage. In some cases they brought a wife with them but this was not always possible in the early years because of the lack of accommodations. Many men came alone, and made acquaintances with young women that had come as servants. The third step was to build or purchase a boat and make agreements with fish merchants to buy their catches. They were then settled and became permanent citizens of their towns. This is the path that the brothers would take for the next few years of their lives, but first of all they had to finish this journey across the sea.

At times during the crossing, nature provided calm waters, leaving a pause in the usual activities of the crew and passengers. Such times thrust the brothers into a journey of introspect that traversed back and forth from security of childhood and home, to the insecurity of manhood and lands afar. George Junior relived the relationship with his parents, and the frustration of knowing so little about his older brother. At times his life was flat and uncertain while at other times his hopes and aspirations made it all worthwhile. One of the things that tormented him was his insistence on leaving his parents behind with worries that could have been avoided, especially taking Joseph with him. He felt responsible for taking him along and wondered how he would adjust to a new world. Even though he felt secure that they would become planters, he hoped that other aspects of life would unfold in a smooth way. He looked forward to marriage and hoped that his responsibility to Joseph would not hinder him from developing a marriage relationship.

Joseph was riddled with loneliness. Even though his brother was with him on this journey, his thoughts were back in Christchurch with his family and friends. He wondered if he should have stayed at home and developed a woodworking business. His father would have been delighted to have had him as a partner. His thoughts many times went back to some of the young ladies and how one of them could be his wife someday. He wondered if he would find new friends in the new land and whether he would have sufficient money to be married. He never discussed these things with George Junior and never expected George Junior to share his thoughts with him.

CHAPTER TWENTY THREE: CRIME AND PUNISHMENT

Both brothers' thoughts were interrupted by the clanging of the evening bell. Although they had access to their own victuals and could eat when they wished, there was an understanding that the meals should be at the same time and that their food should be rationed carefully. Not all of the other passengers were as disciplined. George Junior and Joseph became quite aware of this one foggy morning just as everybody was finding their way to the deck. Two sailors of reckless disposition observed that a couple had left their berths for a while and it looked as if they would be gone for some time. One sailor stood on watch as the other quietly slithered inside the couple's berth. His exit seemed to be unnoticed by all on the ship and the stolen goods were stored in his clothing in a way impossible to see. They nonchalantly made their way back to their berth. The couple returned to escape the fog and for a moment there was no evidence of any interference with their goods. Just shortly later they decided to have a little extra food to start their day, but were quickly horrified by the fact that their victuals were largely depleted. They quickly made their way to the captain and related their experience. At the consent of the captain, the news of the crime spread throughout the ship making the point that if somebody had seen the theft and did not report it, they would receive the same punishment that the thieves would for the crime itself, which would be very severe. Joseph agonized over the matter, trying to banish from his mind that he inadvertently had seen the sailor walk into the couple's berth and return to meet his partner. Questions raced through his mind. Should he tell George Junior? Should he tell anybody? Would it be injustice if he did not? Was not hunger an insignificant punishment compared to the despicable punishment of the crime? Did someone see him just look at the thief then turn away as if to avoid suspicion? He finally made up his mind to tell his brother and get advice on what to do next. That evening before they retired, Joseph related about how he observed the thief and felt very strongly about what he was up to. At least he had another person to help him work through this awful dilemma. Uppermost in both of their minds was the inhumane nature of the punishment.

"Keel Hauling" was used for such crimes. The sailor was tied to a rope that looped beneath the vessel, thrown overboard on one side of the ship, and dragged under the ship's keel to the other side. As the hull was often covered in barnacles and other marine growth, this could result in lacerations and other injuries. This generally happened if the offender was pulled quickly. If pulled slowly, his weight might lower him sufficiently to miss the barnacles but might result in his drowning. If the rope snapped, the captain could conclude that the punishment was not done properly and ordered it carried out again. Alternatives were severe whipping or being covered with boiling fat.

George Junior could not even think of Joseph suffering such torture, and he felt that the right person should receive the punishment. After an intense discussion they made their way to the Captain and Joseph made known what he had seen. The captain hastily sent sailors to the couple's berth to catch them before the food was all consumed. They were caught with foods beyond what had been allocated and there was little they could do to vindicate themselves.

Early in the morning the ropes were secured to the sailors and word went out for all on board to observe a punishment that would discourage any other similar acts. Although they might escape death, the captain read a prayer over them in the same way as if they were going to be executed. In the calm of the morning the sounds of the criminals splashing into the sea left a moment of silence, followed by mumbled prayers. As the ropes were slowly dropped on one side, they were pulled upward on the other, keeping them taut as they made their way underneath the ship. The crowd moved slowly, anxiously awaiting the reappearance of the two criminals before they lost faith that they would survive. Minutes seemed like forever as groups assembled to whisper their hopes and share their viewpoints on how long life could remain without oxygen. Heads turned as the ropes were tightened and two thieves were carefully lifted over the rail. The first glance was of two limp and breathless bodies crumpling on the deck, revealing encounters with barnacles, bruises from hitting the keel, gnaws of unfriendly fish, and unrecognizable faces. Little by little word spread that there were signs of life, followed by a final message that they had survived and would be tended to properly now that the punishment was over. They would, however, be secured in chains lest they try to avenge those that blew the whistle on them. Instead of a cheer that might show resistance to the punishment, the onlookers just drifted away to their berths to ponder what had taken place. For the remainder of the voyage, Joseph fluctuated between feelings of great regret and the reality that he had done the right thing.

Although the unfortunate incident cast a shadow over the journey for a while, other events replaced the dismal mood with mirth, celebrations, periods of calm and sunshine, and the making of new friendships. George Junior and Joseph were fortunate to have conversations with the fishing company representatives which would prove helpful in shortening the process of becoming planters.

The remainder of the voyage was without incident. The final event was a pleasant one as land came into view. There was a pause in all that was taking place as everybody watched the land coming closer and closer. An easy wind took the ship slowly to its destination as shouts of hurrah echoed across its deck. George Junior and Joseph experienced the full realization of where they were and turned their thoughts away from their homeland to this new land that would be theirs for decades to come and to their heirs who would follow in their steps.

CHAPTER TWENTY FOUR: AN UNEXPECTED EVENT

Both brothers were able to obtain a room and a berth on one of the fishing boats, something that they had looked forward to as they crossed the ocean. It was not long before they had their own boat, giving them freedom to search for the best catches along the Twillingate/Fogo shores. The sea was at its best as they sailed the ocean to their new land, but nature's wrath was waiting for them at a moment least expected. It was just after dawn when they set their sails toward their fishing berth off the coast near Fogo, a place where they spent most of their summer. Routine deadens attention to things that happen, lulling the fishermen into the drone of the sails as they flutter in unison. However, it only takes a whiff of wind to nudge a fisherman to a quick alert. Both seemed to feel the movement at the same time. There were no unusual gusts of wind, and no showers of rain, yet the mast seemed to be leaning more than soft winds could push the sails to angle the mast that much. Both George Junior and Joseph stood at the same time to see what was happening, but just as they stood they were thrown toward the starboard and heard the grinding of the keel upon some invisible crag. The boat listed, helped by the mast that was now leaning almost level with the sea. The brothers had to cling to the port side and place their feet upon the starboard side, thankful that no water was coming over the rail. However, they feared for a moment that the boat would fully capsize, but some unseen formation of rocks below them held the boat steady.

They were quick to analyze their predicament, beginning with the awkward position of their stance and with little hope that the situation would correct itself. Dreads abounded: the capsizing of the boat, heavy rain, a storm, running out of food and water, finding no way to reach land, and no other boats passing by. At this point all that they could do was to observe the situation. After an hour or so they began to take turns sleeping. The gunnel was about a foot above water which left a trough that made room for one to lie down. George Junior stretched himself out, lying near Joseph's feet, and amazingly fell asleep. Joseph kept watch in case a vessel might come in sight. It was late afternoon when Joseph took his turn to sleep. The evening was closing in when George Junior noticed that the wind was reaching to gale level making the boat rock slightly to and fro. Joseph was awakened by the movements and took his place beside George Junior to await the increasing wind, fog and rain. Clinging to the gunnel they succumbed to the fact that this was going to be a night of terror. The vessel tossed to and fro at the wishes of the waves. The brothers kept clinging to the gunnel and tried to keep their feet from slipping into the sea. It was in moments like this that they doubted their decisions to leave a safe home in a town that they enjoyed, and the great Priory that inspired them. Most of all their thoughts centered on their parents, George and Elizabeth, their siblings Richard, William, John and Nicholas, their uncle Nicholas and their cousin John who went to

Australia a few years before they came to Newfoundland.

The brothers sat, resigned to spending a long and arduous night, hoping and praying that the boat would not break up. The winds blew harder and the rains became torrential, both of which expressed doom, but what they feared most became their rescue. The mast began to turn upward and the boat slowly became upright. The rising tide lifted the boat from the rocks, the strong wind enabled it to drift into deeper water and as the night went on the storm abated. When daylight broke, they went about making sure that nothing had been damaged. After putting everything in order, they offered a prayer of thanks, and then headed for the next landmark.

CHAPTER TWENTY FIVE: SETTLING IN THE NEW LAND

George Junior who was now over twenty years of age began to feel the desire to marry and settle into a more permanent way of life. His brother Joseph had a number of years yet to pursue marriage, which prolonged the time that George Junior would remain single. However, circumstances changed when he became acquainted with a young woman from Dorset who had come to Twillingate as a servant for a settled married couple with three children. Her name was Mary Patience, in her early twenties, hardworking and well versed in caring for children. She was a very attractive young woman, with a sparkling personality and a social flare about her. George Junior was more rugged which made him wonder how they would relate as husband and wife, seeing that it would take both of their efforts to raise a family in such a harsh environment. The recollection of being raised in Christchurch, and the memories of replacing a brother named

George, still left some measure of inferiority in his life. Also his lineage was one of many siblings and he hoped that Mary would be willing to be a mother to many. All of these things which were going through his mind as they met on various occasions, delayed the moment when he was ready to take the final step. He was coming up to his twenty-fifth birthday when he decided to ask her for her hand in marriage and without hesitating she said, "Yes".

There was no religious denomination or church established in Twillingate at that time, so they were married by a visiting minister. A son was born just a year after the marriage and they called his name George after the father and grandfather. A daughter was born the following year and was named Hannah. Both children were blessings to their home and in spite of the many hardships they enjoyed marriage and children. Joseph, who had settled into their home, became aware that his presence caused awkward moments at times and felt that the time had come for him to live alone.

While they fished in the Twillingate and Fogo areas, they became aware of other places in Newfoundland where fish abounded. One of these was Harbour Grace, a town that was flourishing with activity, including a significant increase in the number of settlers. Joseph visited there and decided that he would settle there as soon as an opportunity came.

The grandparents back in Christchurch were delighted when they received the news that their children had a son and had called him George. It took them back to the day when their firstborn was born and named George. It also awakened the pain that they experienced when their firstborn died. They recalled how they worried about other children dying but when a second son was born they called him by the name of the first son, George. Memories surfaced about how difficult it was when the second George learned about the brother that came before him and how he felt that he was just a replacement. But this was all behind them now, so they rejoiced in the news that not only they had a son George, but now they had a grandson by the same name, a name that was spanning three generations.

There were many times of sorrow in the Verge generations, especially in the deaths of the children that were taken by the diseases of their times. The grandparents wondered what kinds of diseases were present in the new land where their son and grandson were living and if they would receive the care they would need if sickness came to them. Two years after the birth of George, a daughter was born, named Hannah. This news was also sent to the grandparents along with the news that their grandson George was not feeling well but not to worry because there were people in the village who cared for sicknesses of many kinds. Mary knew, however that diphtheria was certainly not under control. A few days after they sent the last message, baby George became very ill and she knew that the dreaded disease had come their way. She was waiting for George Junior to return home one day, hoping that he would see the child alive. It did not turn out that way, for late in the afternoon on a foggy Twillingate day, baby George died. His body was quickly taken from their home just a few hours before her husband returned. In the midst of their heart wrenching grief they held each other and then grasped Hannah as if she would leave them also. The whole episode overcame George Junior as he remembered all that was told him about what took place in the home of his parents some twenty years ago. He was now the one to feel the pain of the death of a firstborn just as his father had felt it decades ago. They wept as they sent a letter to the grandparents, and the grandparents wept as they read it weeks later. The grandparents experienced it all over again; the death of their first born, George and the renaming of a second son, George Junior to keep the namesake alive. Now they felt that the name would cease when their son died. They accepted the situation and turned their attention completely to their young granddaughter, Hannah, who was now just a little over a year old and remained the center of their life, even though they were separated from her by a vast ocean. They looked forward to every letter and followed the new events in their lives. As all of this was taking place, history was turning itself around in an unexpected way. All of the letters up to this time began with the changes in Hannah, but this one began in a different way, bringing new life to the grandparents. They announced that another son was born and that they had named him George, replacing the name of their firstborn son. The grandparents were delighted that, for the fourth time the name George was repeated and hoped that it would continue in the generations to come. In the same way that they followed the growth of Hannah, they would now add the updates of George's life. They continued this for three years at which time they received a message that another son was born and named Richard. Just a few months later news was sent from Elizabeth in Christchurch that Grandfather George had passed away.

The difficult times of raising children and the unceasing appearance of communicable diseases left George and Mary with four renamed children. Their second child, George along with Richard, Patience and William lived many years and raised children in the Twillingate area. Hannah lived to be eighteen years old, during which time three children were born in the family, lived very short lives and were replaced with those former names of Betsy, John and William.

Joseph settled into the town of Harbour Grace, one of the first established towns in Newfoundland. Its mystique developed from the stories that circulated throughout the regions, stories of Pirates having full control of the town, of stories about being caught in the war between America and Britain, and tales of the gaps between the rich and poor. Those stories had faded by the time Joseph settled there in the early nineteenth century and it had become a flourishing town with stable government and established churches. Joseph, already with much experience in the fishing trade, attached himself to settlers that had been there for decades.

One of the first decisions was to find a wife and raise the first Verge family in the town. After he was settled for a while he was very pleased to send a letter to his brother George Junior with news that he would be marrying a young woman named Mary Ann Brown, a spinster in the town. The name George was used again when Joseph's first child was born two years after his marriage to Mary. Other children were born: Richard, William, Frederick, John, Philip, Joseph, Philip and Eli. The first Philip just lived for four years and the next male child was given his name, a confusing tradition that Joseph received from his past. It was just after John was born that Joseph received the news that his brother, George Junior, had died in Twillingate at the age of fifty two.

Joseph was left with memories of the adventures that he and his brother experienced right from the time of the farewell from his parents. He settled in Harbour Grace and died there at the age of sixty nine. His grandsons, Thomas Verge and Selby Duncan Verge, travelled across Newfoundland to Notre Dame Bay. Thomas settled in a little village called Southern Arm. It was there that my father, Joseph Verge, was born and it was there that I was born and spent my childhood.

Epilogue

My goal for this book is that it will become the forerunner of many generation stories. It has been the story of just a few branches of the Verge tree, leaving many others to be explored. When we realize that there are innumerable family names, there is no end to the sequels of this book. I also hope that it has introduced a style of literature that will help ordinary writers put life to their ancestry records.

Manufactured by Amazon.ca
Bolton, ON